Karma is a
Bitch

Volume 2

Angela Hairston

This book is a work of fiction. Name, characters, places and incidents are products of the author's imagination or are used fictitiously. Any resemblance to actual events or locales or persons, living or dead, is entirely coincidental.

Karma is a Bitch
ISBN: 978-0983473237
Copy © 2010 & 2015 & 2016 & 2017 by Angela Hairston
Published by:
Highland Park Publishing
P.O. Box 724651
Atlanta, GA 31139
hairston@highlandparkpublishing.com
www.HighlandParkPublishing.com

Book cover
Copy © 2015 by Angela Hairston
hairston@highlandparkpublishing.com
karmaisabitch@highlandparkpublishing.com

Printed in the United States of America

A Special Dedication

I dedicate this book to my best friend
Barbara Henderson. Thank you for
putting up with me during this
journey. I love you as my sister.

Thank You

My amazing daughter Asia Nelson for always supporting my dream, my beautiful niece Bryanna Black for gracing my cover, the talent photographer Anthony Thomas (ecmanthony@gmail) for the amazing pictures, and Detroit restaurant owner Chief Paul Grosz for welcoming us into Cuisine Restaurant for the photo shoot.

Karma

is a

Bitch

Chapter 1

"Girl I can't believe that motherfucker broke up with you through email," Brittany comment.

"Did you try calling him?" Yolanda asks.

"Hell nay!" I angrily admit.

"That's some fucked up shit. What was his excuse?" Brittany questions.

"Read the email yourself," I suggest.

From: Darrell Hill
Subject: I will always love you
To: Spring Fulton

My Dear Spring,

The last couple of years have been absolutely magical. I truly love you with all my heart. I have never met a woman like you and there will never be another woman in my life time that could compare to you.

Being around you woke up parts of my heart that I never felt before. I found loving you to be as easy as breathing. You made me see that the glass is half full and you being the one that I dreamt of filling it with.

I have not been 100% truthful. I'm not sure how to address this issue. I have been engaged to a childhood girlfriend, since the end of my freshman year in college. I thought she was the one I wanted to spend my live with, until I meet you. The last couple of months I've been working on the best approach to break off our engagement. Unfortunately, life threw a monkey wrench that cannot be avoided.

This was the hardest decision I have ever had to make in my life. I hate to lose you, but I must do the right thing for my unborn son.

I will always be in love with you. You are and always will be my greatest lost.

Darrel

"That motherfucker is engaged and has a baby on the way. Isn't that a bitch," Brittany screeches out.

"This put me in a fucked up situation," I state.

"What do you mean?" Yolanda asks.

"That bitch led me to believe that he wanted me to move in with him this week. Now what am I to do?" I inform.

"The offer still stands if you need a place to stay," Brittany mentions.

"Will Marcus have a problem with it?" I ask.

"He can't tell me who I can and can't have up in this bitch," Brittany says laughing.

"How much will my rent be?" I question.

"Nothing it's all on Marcus," Brittany acknowledge.

"Thanks. It looks like you will have a roommate. After I find a full-time job I'll start looking for my own place," I reply.

"Take your time. I like having you around. It's a good feeling knowing someone else is in this big ass house," Brittany states.

"Thanks. I'm going to head up stairs to unpack," I respond.

"Group hug," Yolanda yells with her arms stretching out.

Chapter 2

I should have known happy endings are not meant for me. I'm sorry that I turned down all my Michigan job offers. I'm hope finding a job in my field will not become an impossible task.

I can wallow in myself pity, but that won't change my situation. I'm going to make the best of the hand I'm dealt. Luckily, I didn't turn down my acceptance to the graduate program at Wayne State University that starts this fall. Guess I'll dip into my savings to buy a dependable used car. From this moment forward it's me against the world.

For the next couple of months I help out at Brittany's boutique, while diligently looking for a job in my field. It took the entire summer to land a part-time accounting job. It's with a large accounting firm in the heart of downtown Detroit. The opportunity has great potential for career growth.

Chapter 3

"Look what the cat dragged in," I comment greeting Brittany upon her arrival home.

"I'm so glad his wife and kids are back at home from their three month European vacation," Brittany announces.

"You didn't like hanging out with big daddy this summer?" I joke.

"Hell nay. Once or twice a week is the most I care to see of him," she declares.

It wouldn't have been that bad if you were not trying to juggle two men!" I joke.

"What have your none dating ass been doing?" she respond switching the subject.

"Restructuring my schedule before school starts in two weeks," I reply.

"That's good, but when are you going to dust the cobwebs off your pussy?" she asks.

"After that shit with Darrell I'm ok for now," I explain.

"A nice stiff dick is the best way to get over a broken heart. You need to get out there and get what you can until that Mr. Right comes along," she instructs.

"Nah, that's not my character," I state.

"Sometimes life experiences can change you. If it wasn't for me wanting to get out of the strip club Marcus would not be in my life," she disclose.

"What made you decide to work at the strip club?" I ask.

"Trust me, stripping was not my first job choose. I had an easy job at the factory making good money. When they shut the plant down it hit me financially hard," she gives details.

"Wasn't there some other jobs out there?" I ask.

"None that paid enough to keep my lifestyle the same," she state

"Why didn't you scale back on your expenses?" I question.

"Once I put myself on a certain level I could not see going back to nothing," she said.

"Were you scared the first time you got on stage?" I quiz.

"Girl I was terrified, but all I kept thinking about was my car being reposed, my utilities being shut off, and moving back to my mother's house," she clarify.

"Did you make much?" I question.

"I did enough to maintain most of my lifestyle," she state.

"I heard stories about what some strippers would do for extra money," I mention.

"Trust, me there are woman with big degrees and excellent paying jobs that are no better than the few that gives the profession a bad name," she harshly state.

"I'm not judging. I'm just curious," I apologetic reply.

"Fortunately the club owner's wife took me under her wing and educated me on how to work the game without being played. She started out as a dancer and became the owner's wife, which got her off the dance floor and gave her the cash flow to open her own restaurant.

She encouraged me to work on a plan that would allow me to become financially independent. She stressed it's best to bang one big payoff instead of banging several small payoffs to reach my goal," she explains.

"So Marcus must be your one big payoff?" I ask.

"Yeah, he turned out to be bigger than I thought!" she comments.

"Is it all worth it?" I ask.

"It was until I realize that I wanted more," she replies.

"What do you mean by that?" I ask.

"As the main mistress his money got me out the strip club and gave me the income to open my boutique. Marcus may satisfy me financially, but sexually he is boring as hell" she explains.

"So, he's married?" I question.

"Yeah, I wouldn't want him any other way. I couldn't put up with him on a daily bases," she describe.

"You seem to have it all. A house, a sharp ass car, your own business, a sugar daddy paying for all your expenses, and a piece of ass on the side," I iterate.

"It all comes with a price. The money alone no longer makes me happy and I'm stuck with Marcus for almost two more years," she state.

"Why are you stuck with him?" I ask.

"I have a few big debits that need to be paid off," she explains.

"Don't you make enough money at the boutique?" I ask.

"I'm secretly purchasing the entire building my boutique is in. Every penny I make at the store is allowing me to save for the deposit needed to secure a mortgage at the end of my contract," she discloses.

"I didn't know that," I mention.

"Nobody knows, especially not Marcus. The rent money from the other stores and not having any large debits will allow me to keep my lifestyle and boot Marcus to the curb," she hints.

"Why not let Shannon pick up the slack?" I question.

"I want this to be mine and mine alone with no strings attached," she state.

"That's the reason why I'm not wasting time working on a relationship," I comment.

"Didn't anybody say a thing about a relationship! You need to do something about the cobwebs growing between your legs," she laughs.

"I'm good," I joke back.

"It's nothing wrong with having someone to release all that built up sexual tense," she comments.

"Is that what Shannon is to you?" I ask.

"No. I love that man and I'm working on taking our relationship to the next step. I really need to step my game up so I can kick Marcus to the curve sooner. Since, I'm the master at pimping I have no doubt that whatever plan I come up with will be brilliant," she declares.

"I can't wait to see you pull this off," I joke.

"What's your excuse for acting like an old maid?" she asks changing the conversation.

"Right now climbing up the corporate ladder is my main concern. I want to become one of the youngest female CFO's at my firm," I inform.

"Let me give you one word of advice," she suggests.

"Go ahead," I reply.

"You better use it or lose it. Get you some dick," she insists.

"Fuck you," I snap.

"Clean the cobwebs from your pussy," she said smacking her lips.

"Fuck you twice," I reply.

"I'll find you a man to break you off. Dick, dick, dick, dick, dick," she chants while walking away.

"Finding a piece of dick is not a priority on my list," I think to myself.

Chapter 4

What beautiful weather for a late September evening. Brittany and I decide to fire up the grill and chill on the patio. What a nice way to enjoy two delicious T-Bone steaks with a bottle or two of Cabernet Sauvignon red wine.

After getting the fire just right for the vegetables there's a knock on the backyard gate door. Behold to my surprise its Brittany's mystery man. This is the first time I get the chance to meet the infamous Shannon. I'm more shocked to see her taking the chance of having him over knowing that crazy ass Marcus rides down the street at times.

"Shannon, this is my girl Spring," Brittany said introducing the brown skinned slimly built man.

"Nice to meet you," he respond smiling and showing off his dimples.

"I finally meet the face behind the man that Brittany is always talking about," I joke as she pinches my arm.

"So that's the college girl that lives with you," he whispers to Brittany as Spring attend to the grill.

"Yes. She's the one I wanted to introduce to your boy," she comments as they continue whispering to each other.

"Damn, he would like her," he state.

"Why didn't he come?" she ask.

"He thought it was your girl Cherry," he answer.

"I don't deal with that stink bitch like that," she admits.

"Does your girl know you're trying to hook her up with my boy?" he question.

"No. She's completely blind to the fact that she needs a man. All those text books have clouded her judgment. I think your boy would treat her right and break her out of the nerdy shell she's hiding in," she admits.

"It's time he stop dealing with them bucket heads," he agree.

"I have another steak in the house if you want to stay for dinner," she offers before walking back into the house.

"I know I'm taking a chance of Marcus riding down on me, but it might be time to stop this charade. I'm going to let the cards play out and see what happens. However, if it goes down Marcus will be the one shit out of luck," Brittany thinks to herself as she walks to the front closet to get another lawn chair.

"I can't believe this trick has another motherfucker over her house," Marcus says to himself as he cruises down the block and notices a black Range Rover in Brittany's driveway.

As Brittany closes the closet door she observes Marcus pulling up in the driveway. She snatches up her cell phone from the hallway table and rush upstairs to hide. She quickly cut the phone's ringer off and begins texting.

"Marcus just pulled up," she text Spring and Shannon.

"Where r u?" I text.

"In ur closet," she text.

Since, the front door is unlocked Marcus lets himself in.

"He just entered the house," she text to us.

He didn't hear any movement downstairs so he head upstairs.

"He's walking up the stairs," she text us.

"Need me to come in," Shannon text back.

"No," she text.

Marcus silently tries creeping up the stairs to bust Brittany in the bed with another nigger. He flings her bedroom door open, but to his surprise there is nothing to catch. So, he checks her bathroom, under the bed, and in the closet. He rushes down the hallway to check the other bedrooms.

"He's coming down the hall," she text us.
"I'm coming in," Shannon text.
"Don't," she text.
"He's in the spare bedroom," she text.

After thoroughly checking under the bed and the closet, he passes through the bathroom to enter Spring's bedroom only to find it empty.

"He's coming through the bathroom," she text.
"Make some noise," she text us.
"Talk real loud," she text.

As he holds his hand on the closet door knob he hears a male voice coming from the backyard. He's unable to make out the voices through the closed windows. With his adrenalin rushing at the idea of busting her cheating he heads downstairs.

"He's running down the stairs," she text.
"Think he is heading outside," she text seconds before he emerges from the patio door.

"Where is Brittany?" Marcus grimly demands.
"She went to check on her mother," I answer.
"Your girl said your checking on your mom," Shannon text.
"Stop lying, her car is in the driveway," Marcus angrily state.
"Yolanda picked her up," I lie.
"She said your cuz picked you up," Shannon text.

"Why the hell didn't she drive herself?" Marcus grills.

"It was an emergency," I answer.

"Emergency with ur mom," Shannon text.

"Why didn't you go?" Marcus asks.

"You have a lot of questions! Why don't you call her yourself?" I answer being annoyed with his line of questions.

"He's calling," Shannon text.

"Where the hell are you?" was the message Marcus left on her voicemail seconds before Brittany calls back.

"Hey, I'm at the hospital," Brittany states before Marcus can say anything.

"Why are you whisper," Marcus asks.

"The doctors just walked in the room and I need to hear what they have to say. I'll call you later," Brittany informs.

"Go take care of your mother and call me later," Marcus replies trying to sound concerned. He turns around and walks out the backyard without saying a word.

Brittany watches from an upstairs window as Marcus drive down the block. She returns to the patio once she is sure he's not returning. As much as she wants this to end she knows timing is everything.

"Was that my competition?" Shannon question Brittany when she comes out the house.

"There's no competition between the two of you," she answers.

"Explain to me why you keep that buster around?" he quiz.

"He holds the lease on my store and I'm just waiting until the lease is up," she confesses.

"How long before the lease is up?" he asks.

"Just under two years," she reveals.

"Just move your shop to another location!" he suggests.

"It's not that easy," she discloses.

"Make me understand," he instructs.

"We'll talk about that another time," she declares.

"Ok, this game can't go on to long without someone getting hurt. Trust me I don't expect it to be either of us," he command.

"That was some retired ass shit," I interject trying to break the dark cloud that Marcus seems to leave.

"You should have been in my shoes," she suggests.

"Or do you mean my closet," I state while giggling.

"That man has no idea who I am!" Shannon comment.

"No," Brittany replies.

"That's some funny shit. The player is being played," he laughs.

Chapter 5

After the baby's birth I anxiously pace around the hospital room waiting for every to leave. Both our parents are in from Michigan and several of her sorority sisters showed up. We have not had one moment alone since, Connie went into labor.

"I know you don't think I'm signing that boy's birth certificate. That's not my kid. He's to fucking light," I blurt out the moment the last person leaves.

"He's yours," Connie replies in a soft sweet tone.

"You must be kidding! Those piercing blue eyes! He is damn near bleach white," I state.

"He will darken up" she explains trying to play stupid.

"Who the hell is the boy's real father?" I demand.

"Are you trying to accuse me of cheating?" she quarrels.

"Hoe, your ass gave birth to the proof?" I assert.

"I know you're not calling me a hoe. I made one mistake of sleeping with a white boy, but that doesn't compare to what your ass put me through," she spat.

"You got a lot of nerves blaming your affair on me. Do you have any idea that I gave up all my dreams thinking I'm going to be a father," I disputes.

"You mean you had to give up Spring! Yeah, don't stand there looking all shocked. I have known about her for years. I thought you would have left your campus freak alone once you graduated. How dare you choose to introduce your new life to that tramp first! I found the pictures at your apartment of the two of you hanging out in Chicago. Then you had the nerves taking me to the same cheap ass places you took her! We both made mistakes. I forgive you for your faults, so you need to do the same," she throws back at him.

"You are definitely right about one thing. I truly regret giving up Spring. I assumed I was doing right by my child," I declare.

"Now that everything is out. We can put that all in the past and work on our marriage for the baby's sake," she suggests.

"There would not have been a marriage if you had not lied about your pregnancy!" I lash out.

"You promised for better or worse. This is the worst it could get. So put on your big boys underwear and deal with it," she insist.

"You think I'm a motherfucking fool!" I yell.

"No, you're a good man that always does the right thing. I knew you wouldn't disappoint your mother, by choosing that tramp over me," she acknowledges.

"It was Spring that I wanted to marry, have kids by, and build a life with. I should have stood my ground and followed my heart," I swear.

"Were the hell do you think you're going?" she demands.

"I'll be moved out of the house by tomorrow," I announce.

"Please, stay until our parents go back to Michigan. You just need some time to think this over," she pleads.

"Fuck that shit. I'm filing for divorce," I angrily state as I storm out the room.

Damn all my calls are going straight to Spring's voicemail. I'm not anticipating seeing our parents when I make it home. I walk through the front door, head straight to the master bedroom locking the door behind me.

"Son, is everything ok?" my father asks from the other side.

"Please go away," I reply.

"Let me in. I'm not going away!" he forcefully state.

"Please stop knocking," I yell out while throwing my clothing on the bed.

"Baby, this is your mother. Please let us in. I'm worried," she begs.

"Only my father," I order allowing him to enter and locking the door behind him.

"What's going on?" he ask.

"The baby is not mines. I know you noticed the skin color," I inform.

"The baby could darken up or have traits from someone in her family," he suggests.

"She admitted the baby's real father is white. I ruined everything," I grumble.

"Everything is not ruined. You are married and Connie loves you," he said.

"Dad, I only married her because of the baby. I'm still in love with Spring," I admit.

"Why did you go through with the wedding?" he ask.

"I didn't want to disappoint you and mom," I confess.

"You would not have disappointment me. As far as your mother, she would have gotten over it. Take some time and think this through," he proposes.

"I have lost enough time. Connie knows that I will be out of here before she comes home from the hospital. I also, informed her that I'm filing for divorce," I disclose.

"I'm behind any decision you make, but you need to be the one to tell your mother," he commend.

"Your right," I agree allowing him to unlock the bedroom door.

"Is everything ok?" Connie's parents ask.

"You need to talk with Connie," I instruct closing the door after my mother enters the room.

I sit her down on the bed to explain. She silently weeps at the news as she watches me pack my clothes. She feels bad for my situation, but is more hurt the baby not her grandchild.

Chapter 6

"Man why don't you come to the bar with me tonight?" I ask.

"Shannon, correct me if I'm wrong. You're hanging with your girl tonight," Jason replies.

"I am, but a couple of her girls are going to be there and it would be nice to have another guy in the group," I respond.

"You're still trying to hook me up with one of her sorry ass girls? That last bitch busted out my car windows. Besides hanging out at a strip club with her whack ass friends is a waste of my time," Jason calls out.

"We're not meeting up at a strip club and this is a completely different group of women. Besides, I'm not trying to hook you up. I just want to hang out with my boy," I state.

"So, am I the only other male going," Jason ask.

"Maybe," I reply.

"You can stop playing me for a fool. Last week you tried to get me to go over to her house. Now tonight you want me to hang with you, your girl, and her friends! What the hell is up?" Jason questions.

"Ok, I have to admit I was trying to hook you up," I reveal.

"Man, I will never fuck with another stripper friend of Brittany's," Jason state.

"This one is not a stripper. Matter of fact she's in college, fine, and holds a real job," I announces.

"You're telling me that for what?" Jason questions.

"Brittany thinks you two will make a cute couple," I disclose.

"Hell nay. Not after dealing with that bitch Cherry. I don't want to meet anymore of her stripper ass friends," Jason declares.

"She's not a stripper. She's a college girl," I maintain.

"Stripper, college it' doesn't make a difference. So, far all of Brittany girls that are not hoes or strippers have been butt fucking ugly," Jason stress.

"Trust me man, this girl is fine as hell," I encourage.

"That's ok. I'm doing fine on my own," Jason state.

"She makes your best look like trash," I announce.

"Yeah, yeah, yeah. You can drop it, because I'm not interested. When has your girl every hung around quality chicks," Jason claim.

"She's a friend of her cousin Yolanda," I respond.

"Hell nay, I met her before. That doesn't explain why she's hanging out with your girl and not her stiff ass cousin!" Jason comment.

"She's letting her stay with her, while she works on her master degree," I reply.

"I got the point that she is educated, but she must be ugly as hell if she needs your help to hook her up with a man," Jason said.

"Trust me she's fine," I state.

"If she's fine, educated, working, and doesn't have a man she must be a crazy ass bitch," Jason assumes.

"From what Brittany explains to me she had her heart broken from a square ass college boy. Come on, it want hurt to check her out!" I add.

"I think I'll pass that one up. I don't have time to deal with a square ass woman that is probable still suffering from a broken heart," Jason iterates.

"Ok, man. Don't say shit when one of our other boys starts sporting her around," I reply.

Chapter 7

I have several excellent reasons to celebrate this weekend. I got an "A" my big mid-term exam paper, less than three months on the job I'm promoted to a full-time internal auditor's position, and my girls Hattie and Carrie are coming in town for the weekend.

Brittany is cool with everyone staying at the house. A girl's weekend is long overdue. Our first stop tonight is Floods Bar and Grill, which is one of Detroit's favorite after work spots.

We're sitting along the bar facing the dance floor and the stage. Blue Hawaiians is always the best drink to wash away the work week stress. We picked a good night for a live performance. An exceptionally talented locale artist Korey Barksdale and the 313 Band is showing out.

"Liquor goes well with your group," Brittany comment.

"Why you say that?" I ask.

"Carrie is dancing on beat, you socializing, and Yolanda's jokes are actually funny. You and your girls are surprisingly not as square tonight," Brittany admits.

"We are never square. Maybe you need to hang with us more often. You might learn something," I state.

"I doubt if I learn anything. Hanging with you all is not a bad idea, but not this weekend," she state as I notices Shannon entering the bar.

"What up Spring and Yolanda?" Shannon greets as he hugs Brittany.

"Shannon, these are my girls Hattie and Carrie," I introduce.

"Nice to meet you," he state.

"What happen to your boy," Brittany whisper in his ear.

"It was a no go. This after work crowd is not my thing. Are you ready to go?" he asks.

"Let me give Spring the car keys and valet ticket," she responds.

For the next couple of hours we are having a great time especially since, several of the old men put all our food and drinks on their tabs. As I walk towards the back of the bar to the bathroom, I recognize a couple of Darrell's frat brothers. When I exit the bathroom I realize they are his frat brothers. I'm shocked to be standing face to face with Darrell before I was able to turn and walk away.

"I tried calling you. I left several voicemails, as well as text messages," Darrell state.

"I know I deleted them all," I inform him.

"Why would you do that? Sorry, I understand why you would not want to return my calls, but I really need to talk to you," he try explaining.

"Another woman's husband and baby daddy has nothing to say to me!" I reply.

"Hear me out!" he request.

"No," I snap as I turn to walk away.

"You once said you would love me forever," he blurts out while grabbing my hand.

"You once said the same thing, but that didn't stop you from marrying another woman," I harshly respond snatching my hand away.

"I only married her because she claims to be having my baby," he expresses jumping in front of me.

"Congratulation on your child and your marriage," I say.

"I'm not married anymore," he state.

"She got wise and left your ass," I comment while smacking my lips.

"No, I left her. She revealed knowing about us and trapping me with the baby when she realized my heart belonged to you," he explains.

"So you were fucking the both of us?" I question.

"I was stupid, but you are the one I really wanted. The baby turned out not to be mine. It came out bleached white with blond hair and blue eyes. She knew it was a 50/50 chance on the baby's paternity but was hoping it was mine," he rambles on.

"I guess I was the only one in your love triangle not sleeping around," I stress.

"I may have loved her at one time, but I have always been in love with you. I hope there's a chance for me to make it up to you?" he asks.

"When hell freezes over twice. I unconditionally gave you everything. My heart, my loyalty, and my virginity. You took them, misused them, shit on them, and threw them out like trash," I state.

"Baby, I love you and don't want to live without you!" he claims.

"That sounds like a problem that I'm not willing to help you with," I angrily reply throwing a drink sitting on the bar in his face and walking away.

"Let's go," I request after making it back to my girls.

"Is everything ok?" Carrie asks.

"I just ran into that asshole Darrell," I reply.

"You want to head home?" Yolanda asks.

"No. I'm not going to let him ruin my weekend," I respond.

"Time to blow this place and hit the next one," Hattie says.

Chapter 8

"Is your ass going to help me fold my clothes?" Brittany asks.

"What's in it for me?" I question.

"Why does it have to be something in it for you?" she asks.

"As I was taught by a dear friend, you never give any of your time if it doesn't profit you in the end," I answer.

"Just making sure you are absorbing my wisdom. I'll be willing to share my pitcher of lime margarita," she responds.

"Thanks again for letting everyone stay over this past weekend," I reply climbing on to her bed to help fold clothes.

"It was a pleasure. A weekend without Marcus is always a treat," she admits.

"So I take it you and Shannon had a good time," I comment

"We had a great time and it got me thinking about my future. I'm so ready to kick Marcus to the curb," she admits.

"Why don't you? I'm making a lot more money and can help with the household expenses," I offer.

"It's much more complicated than that!" she state.

"You sure it's nothing I can do to help?" I ask.

"The problem is the store is leased in Marcus name that's why the owner rents it to me so cheap. I'm buying the building as a land contract under a business name," she discloses.

"It seems to me it wouldn't be a problem putting it in your name since you are purchasing the building," I state.

"The owner of the building is Marcus' brother and he has no idea it's me he's selling it to. If he finds out before closing I'm sure that could fuck everything up. I want this transaction with the building to go as smooth as possible. After that I don't give a fuck how the breakup goes," she explains.

"You're not scared of him acting a fool?" I question.

"He has a wife and several other hoes to focus his attention on. Besides my relationship with Shannon will no longer be a well-kept secret," she suggests.

"I think you need to let Shannon know what's going on. Keeping secrets can blow up in your face," I mention.

"Your right, I owe that to him," she agrees.

"Talking about shit blowing up in someone's face. Did I tell you that I ran into Darrell's black ass at Flood's?" I brought up.

"No. I hope you cussed his ass out?" she asks.

"I did that and threw a drink in his face," I admit.

"I would have spit in his eye," she adds.

"He's been blowing up my voicemail and my text messages. Talking about how sorry he is, that he's still in love with me, and he only married her because he thought he was doing right by the baby that turned out not to be his," I inform.

"Get the fuck out of here," she responds.

"That motherfucker got his pay back. She was messing around with a white boy and the baby came out with blue eyes and blond hair," I disclose.

"That's what his ass gets," she state.

"Pay back is a bitch," is the last thing I remember saying before my fourth margarita kicked in.

Chapter 9

"Thanks for coming by so fast," Brittany said upon Shannon's arrival.

"You sounded serious," Shannon reply.

"I need to explain the Marcus situation," I state.

"I'm all ears," he replies.

For the next couple of hours we sit up talking. I divulge the full story about Marcus and why I put up being one of his sidekicks. I explain why breaking it off with him at this time is not a wise business move. I express my feeling towards him and how I want a future with him.

"In a strange sort of way I understood your motives. I can front you the money!" he offers feeling empathy for her.

"No. The money might change the dynamics of your relationship," I decline.

"Babe, I'm glad you opened up and told me everything. This lets me know that there is a future for us. I will be patient and let this play out. Don't hesitate to tell me if you need some muscle," he state respecting her wishes. "The fact that she turned down my financial support proves she loves me for me and not my money.

"Thanks for understanding," I respond with a hot passionate kiss.

"You know you're starting something that you have to finish," he mentions.

"I never start anything I can't finish," I reply leading him up stairs.

When we reached me bedroom Spring is still laying across the bed dead sleep. It doesn't make any sense trying to wake her drunken ass up. We leave her there and proceed down the hall to the spare bedroom.

"Come over me my Betty Boop," he request while sitting on the end of the bed.

"Why do I have to be Betty Boop," I reply while dimming the light before walking over to him.

"If you were taller than you would be my Jessica Rabbit," he jokes.

"That's just as bad," I state.

"Baby, you have a body so flawlessly that it could only have been created by a great artist," he responds while cupping her breast.

"I can accept that answer," I reply engaging him in a deep tongue kiss.

I grab her waist and lowering us both to the bed. I hold her ass as we scoot further up the bed. We continue kissing as I squeeze on her ass.

I sit up on my knees to help him remove his shirt. Then I removed my top revealing my perfectly shaped breast. I lower my chest close enough for him to hold tightly to one breast and place the other breast in his mouth. I bit my bottom lip while enjoying him sucking on my breast.

I take pleasure in feeling her hard nipples sliding down my chest as she makes her way south. I prop up my butt with my legs up so she could remove my pants and underwear. She grabs hold of my penis and began sucking on the head. I lay back moaning as I allow her magical tongue to drive me sexually crazy.

I softly kiss the tip of his penis as I finish sucking it. I want him so bad that I quickly take my panties off, roll a condom over his penis, straddle over him, and engulfing his fully erect dick within my wet pussy. The ecstasy I feel as every inch of his dick slides inside of me. I hold on to my breast and relish in the synchronize strokes from our bodies.

"Damn this pussy is good," he moans out.

"My pussy craves your dick," I moan back.

"That's it ride the shit out of my dick," he demand while holding onto my waist.

"This is a ride I never want to get off," I acknowledge.

I had her get on all four so I can beat that pussy up doggie style. With a firm grip on her waist I move her body closer as a ram my dick into her wet soft pussy. I can feel her body lightly tensing up with every inch of my dick's deep penetration.

He has no idea that I fantasy about his dick every time I'm with Marcus. That is the only way I can force myself to sexually be with that asshole.

"Baby, I love to feel your skin against mine," I inform as his arms wrap around my stomach to cupping my breast.

"I also love my skin against yours," he reveals.

"That's it," I shout.

"Who's, dick do your pussy want?" he ask.

"My pussy wants yours," I reply.

"Lay on your back," he order.

As she lay on her back I use my arms to drape her legs up and over my shoulder. I cover her legs with my arms rendering her totally helpless as I thrust my dick in and out of her pussy. Feeling her legs shiver on my down strokes makes me want her pussy more.

With a tight grip on the headboard I moan loudly as I enjoy every deep stroke of his dick inside of my pussy. His dick feels so good inside of me, causing my legs to shake uncontrollable.

"Why you stop," I ask when he pulls releasing the hold on me legs.

"Your shit is so good that I need another condom," he admits as he quickly peels the filled one off and replaces it with a new one.

We hold each other tightly climaxing together after forty minutes in every position we could think of and three condoms.

"Baby, I'll be glad when this foolishness is over and I can have you to myself," he mentions.

"Mentally you do have me to yourself," I inform.

"I physically want you to myself," he state.

"You have no idea how many times I play the fake period," I mention.

"What's the fake period?" he asks.

"Every time I do not want to have sex with him a put on at maxi pad and pretend I'm bleeding," I inform.

"How do you get him to believe that?" he ask.

"After my mom got sick I came up with a bogus family genetic thyroid disorder. He's so stupid he never checks," I reveal.

"You are a character. Should I watch out for that trick?" he question.

"No, my body craves your touch" I admit.

"I'm glad I didn't meet the bogus you. I love the real you," he reply.

"I love you too," I reply back.

Chapter 10

Around four in the morning Marcus is heading home from hanging with his boys. He decides to go out his way to drive down Brittany's block. He notices the same black Range Rove from the last time he popped over is parked in the driveway. So, he chooses to see if the nigger is really there for Spring. He parks a couple of houses down.

"Why the hell are you calling so late," Brittany quietly responds answering her phone.

"Hey, I'm in the neighborhood. I should be there in ten minutes," he quickly announces before hanging up the phone.

"I'll see if that motherfucker is there for you or Spring. How the fuck is one of my jump offs going to cheat on me?" he mumbles to himself as he sit staring at the house waiting to see if he observe any movement.

Chapter 11

"Oh, shit," I said transitioning into not getting busted mode.

In the dark I run down the hall to my bedroom. I'm happy to see that Spring must have gotten up sometime during the night and went to her bedroom. I pull down the covers on my side of the bed only, take a hoe bath, sprayed body mist on, put on a pad, slide into a flannel pajama set, and place a head scarf on to hide my sweated out hair. I rush to meet him at the front door before he can ring the doorbell and wake anyone up.

"Hey, baby," I greet swinging the front door open and realizing he's sloppy drunk.
"Whose truck is that in your driveway," he slurs out.
"Spring's boyfriend must be over," I swiftly answer.
"You let your girl disrespect your house like that!" he sternly state.
"For one she's a grown woman, for two how dare you question what goes on in my house, for three you only stop by because you

thought the driver of the truck was with me," I snap back pointing my finger in his face.

"No, no, it's not like that," he stutters while closing the door behind him.

"Isn't this your wifey's nights," I suggest hoping that would get him to leave.

"Can't a man break his own rules to spend some time with his number one girl?" he asks while heading upstairs.

"You haven't in all these years," I nervously say hoping to stop him from going upstairs.

"Better late than never," he replies as he rushes into my bedroom.

"I hope you find what you're looking for," I state as he franticly search my room.

When he couldn't find any traces of a man being in my bedroom he head down the hall to check out the spare bedroom. I decide not to stop him and let the shit go down. On his way down the hall a glimmer of light reflecting from under the bathroom door as someone enters from one of the bedrooms.

"Baby, come back to bed," Shannon yell out thinking it's Brittany in the bathroom.

"Go back to sleep," Spring answer back assuming Brittany and Shannon both are in the spare bedroom and he's talking in his sleep.

Marcus stops in his tracks feeling stupid assuming he was going to catch me cheating. He turns around and head towards my bedroom. I'm caught off guard by how perfect that played out.

"What the hell is that you have on," he question as he run his hand across my crouch.

"A pad," I sarcastically answer.

"You on your period again?" he question.

"How many times do I have to tell you that I have a thyroid problem," I reply reminding him of the lie I been telling for years.

"Guess I have to settle for a good blow job," he state while climbing into my bed fully dressed.

The thought of sliding his dick between my lips with Shannon sleeping down the hall is totally disgusting. I'll undress him extremely slow.

By the time I finally get his boxers off he has fallen into a deep drunken sleep. I pull some lubricating gel from my nightstand and rub it around the top half of his dick and his inner thighs. Knowing in the morning he will be too hung over to tell that the dried up sticky substance is not from his semen.

This can play out to my advantage. Once he begins to snoring extremely loud I gently slid out the bedroom and down the hall.

I quietly wake Shannon up to explain my situation and plans to him. I demand that he brings Spring up to speed in the morning. He falls back to sleep chuckling about me being in a flannel pajama set and wearing a pad. I creep back into the bedroom and climb back in bed next to Marcus like nothing has happened.

Chapter 12

The next morning I'm in the kitchen fixing a breakfast suitable for a person with a hangover. I'm truly surprise to see Shannon entering the kitchen, knowing Marcus' car is parked in front of the house. After the last run in with Marcus, this is a very daring move for Brittany. I can only assume that she knows what she's doing.

"Good morning," Shannon says as he enter the kitchen.

"Good morning to you. Would you like something to eat," I offer.

"From the look on your face I can tell you're shocked to see me," he mentions.

"If that's what you want to call it," I reply.

"Brittany wants me to bring you up to speed," he state while fixing a plate.

"Explain," I command.

"Because of the awkward situation that arouse last night she decided the count down on kicking Marcus to the curb must start today. She came up with a plan, but she needs our help," he continues to giving details.

"I'll do anything to get that buster out your life," I reply.

"We need to make him feel extremely uncomfortable around us," he responds.

"How are you going to do that?" I ask.

"We need to act like a couple when he comes downstairs. She also wants me to strike up a small conversation," he state.

"What the hell would you talk to him about?" I ask.

"She wants me to pretend that I'm a friend of his wife's stepbrother. I'm not sure how that is supposed to make him feel uncomfortable?" he answers with a question.

"I get it. He can't afford for his wife finding out about her. To keep his secret from coming out it might cause him to avoid coming over whenever he see's your truck in the driveway," I state.

"Were you able to bring Spring up to speed?" Brittany quickly asks as she enters the kitchen.

"Yes," he answers as we hear Brittany's bedroom door open and Marcus descending down the stairs.

"So what's going on?" Marcus asks in a grim voice as he enters the kitchen.

"Good morning baby," Brittany greets acting like nothing is wrong.

"Who is that?" Marcus questions.

"Marcus this is my friend Shannon," I easily roll off my tongue with a smile on my face.

"I seen you a couple of weeks ago when we were on the patio. By the way you look very familiar," Shannon mention.

"I doubt if you know me," Marcus state.

"You almost resemble my man Junebug's brother-in-law," Shannon adds.

"Sorry, I don't have any brother-in-laws," Marcus demand.

"Well it's nice meeting you," Shannon said holding his hand out for a shake.

"Same here," Marcus reply refusing to shake his hand.

"Would you like to sit down and eat with us," I offer.

"No thanks. Brittany, can we talk in the other room!" Marcus request while walking out the kitchen.

"What do you want to talk about?" Brittany asks meeting Marcus in the foyer.

"Nothing now. I can't take the chance of Junebug finding out. He would definitely tell his sister," Marcus answers.

"Maybe it's time for everything to be out in the open. I'm tired of only seeing you once or twice a week," she lies.

"I explained my situation from the start. You know I'm not going anywhere until the last kid is out the house," he state.

"That excuse would be acceptable if you still weren't having more kids with her," she replies.

"No, no ,no. It's not like that. I love you," he claims.

"You have been telling me that for years, but I'm still your dirty little secret. What more do you want from me?" she respond.

"Baby I'm so sorry for making you feel that I don't appreciate the scarifies you take to be with

me.   I really need to get out of here," he
mention.

"So you're trying to rush off to avoid this
conversation!" she reply.

"I have to get home and put the fire out
from me not coming home last night," he
explains.

"Just go," she replies dismissing him.

"I hate to leave like this.   I'll make it up to
you next week," he claims as Brittany closes the
door behind him.

"Thanks," Brittany says as she returns to
the kitchen.

"You're welcomed.   I'm going back to bed,"
I respond while exiting the kitchen.

"That simple minded motherfucker bought
that?" Shannon asks.

"Every word.   From now on whenever he
sees your truck he will be scared to stop by.
Hooking Spring up with your boy would be
perfect, since you both drive black Rovers,"
Brittany responds.

"I tried, but he truly believes that it's one of
your girls from the strip club," he mentions.

"I'll handle this.   By this evening he will be
begging you to hook him up," she insists.

"After this morning I have no doubt that you
can pull anything off.   What's the rush?" he
agrees with a question.

"Her old boy is trying to weasel his way
back and I refuse to let that mother fucker stomp
all over her heart again.   Just have Jason over
to your house around 6 pm," she suggests.

"What do you have planned?" he asks.

"Don't worry about that. Trust me he will be willing to dumb his date for the concert on Thanksgiving," she inform.

Chapter 13

"Hey Shannon," I yell running around to climb into the driver's seat of Brittany's car.

"Hey you," he reply while patting Brittany on the butt as she rush into his house.

"Damnnnn. Who is that?" Jason asks as Spring pulls off.

"That's her girl Spring," he answers.

"I have never seen her at the strip club," Jason mentions.

"You wouldn't because she's not a stripper. That's the college girl I tried to set you up with," he answers with a devilish grin on his face.

"Damn she is fine as hell," Jason admits.

"I told you so," he replies.

"Man I thought you were trying to hook me up with a booger bear. I've seen a couple of her girls. Hell, most of them need to wear a bag over their heads," Jason declares.

"Why, would I do some shit like that. She's hot, single, educated, and has a real job," he adds.

"It doesn't add up. There has to be something wrong with her. There's no way someone that fine should be single. Tell me the truth man? Is she crazy or something?" Jason asks.

"Like I told you before she's cool but a little square," he mentions.

"What do you mean by square?" Jason asks.

"If she's not at school or work she has her head stuck in one of her text books," he respond.

"I know someone has to be tapping that ass," Jason state.

"Brittany said she hasn't dated since her boyfriend from college broke her heart. If I'm not mistaking he's the only guy she has ever been with," he discuss.

"Ohh, if he busted that cherry then broke her heart she must be one of those extremely bitter chicks!" Jason claims.

"Brittany thinks all she needs is someone to treat her right," he suggest.

"See if you can still hook that up for me," Jason request.

"I'll talk to my girl," he responds.

"Cool," Jason reply.

Later that evening when Brittany comes home she finds Spring snuggling. Not with a man but with a pile of text books. She figures this will be the best time to proposition her about going out with Jason.

"Hey did you notice that guy on Shannon's porch?" Brittany asks.

"What about him?" I respond with a question.

"He thinks you're hot and would like to meet you," she says.

"I don't have time to deal with another ass hole," I inform.

"He's a sweetheart that will give you anything you ask for," she adds.

"I'm not looking for a sugar daddy. Oops, in his case a sugar boy," I state.

"What the hell is a sugar boy?" she laughs.

"He looks young as hell," I state.

"His twenty-one or twenty-two. You're a hot mess calling someone young. You could pass as a high school student," she jokes.

"What's the real reason behind you trying to set me up?" I address.

"Ok, it's a favor for Shannon. His boy asked him about hooking y'all up. Besides you deserve to have someone treat you like a queen every now and then. I know for a fact that he has no fiancé, girlfriend, or baby mama hiding out there," she admits.

"I'm not looking for a man," I respond.

"It wouldn't hurt to have someone to take you out from time to time. You really need to loosen up and get some dick," she state.

"Here you go with this dick shit!" I slam back.

"Good dick is the best stress reliever," she throws back.

"A good workout releases my stress," I state.

"Trust me. Combine the two, I bet it will help you take the world by surprise," she claims.

"I still think you have another reason for trying to hook us up," I allege.

"Seriously, I don't care to socialize with the other guys' women and it would be nice to have my girl with me," she insist.

"You don't have to pimp me out to get me to hang with you two," I argue.

"I'm going to need your companionship this Thursday," she request.

"You know that I hate celebrating the holidays," I remind her.

"I know how much you love Kem's music. They have a bunch of tickets to his concert at the Fox Theater. The only thing you have to be his boy's date for the evening," she admits.

"Damn. I guess for the sake of seeing Kem, I can put up with him for one night," I accept.

Chapter 14

"Is that what you're going to wear?" Brittany asks.

"It's easy for you, since you have a small department store compared to my selection," I respond.

"It's not the amount of clothes but the way you put your outfit together. You need to accentuate your assets," she state while going through my closet. "Your closet is boring as hell. Everything looks like you work a nine to five job twenty four hours a day."

"Thanks to my tuition bill I don't have spare change lying around," I reply.

"Where is your black low rider jean? Where's that sweater I gave for Christmas last year?" she ask.

"Right here, but the sweater is too small," I respond.

"This is sad. You are clueless to fashion. The sweater is meant to fit that way. When I get back with some accessories you better be dressed," she declares.

"Told, you the sweater is too small. It barely covers my belly button and my boobies are hanging out. Why all the black?" I complain.

"Shut up and put this jewelry and belt on," she instruct as she rambles through my shoes collection.

"How the hell is this sweater supposed to accentuate my cheap ass jeans?" I question.

"I was talking about your shape. If I had a pair of tits likes yours my ass would be extremely dangerous. Put these black boots on with my mink jacket and bring your ass on," she replies heading down the hallway.

"I don't feel comfortable," I complain.

"You look sexy ass hell and that's all that matters," she comments.

"It's not like I'm going on a real date," I grumble following her down the stairs.

"Real date or not you should always look your best," she said while heading to answer the front door.

Shannon walks in with his boy. At least his brown skinned ass is not hard on the eyes. He's looks to be six feet tall and thanks to his top I can tell he works out.

Spring this is Jason and Jason this is Spring," Shannon introduce.

"Do they call you Spring because you're a spring of fresh air?"Jason remarks.

"No. They call me Spring because it my legal name," I snap.

"Uhmm, Spring that is my favorite season," Jason replies as his eyes examine me up and down.

"If I got paid every time a man said that lame ass line I would be a millionaire by now," I suggest.

"Off to a rough start. I hope it gets better," Brittany whisper to Shannon.

"Me too," Shannon whisper back as they head for the truck.

"If it wasn't for Kem's concert I would not be wasting my time on this shame of a date. The ride downtown would be pleasant if the man stop staring at my chest. I told her this sweater was too little," I thinking to myself.

"Acting nice want kill you," Brittany text from the front seat.

"Didn't realize I wasn't being nice," I text back.

"Be nice for me," she text.

"Only for you," I text back.

We pull in front of the theater at the valet parking. Jason rushes around the truck to open my door. He has the nerve to slightly hold me around the waist as we walk through the entrance. If it wasn't for him having the tickets I would have pushed his hand away. Let me be nice for Brittany sake. I put on a fake smile while posing for pictures and stand in the lobby as he talks with his boys.

"Thanks for coming. Now you get the chance to see how the other women treat me," Brittany mentions.

"Who is that fine ass guy over there?" I ask.

"The one with the curly hair and gray eyes?" she asks.

"That's who you should have hooked me up with," I suggest.

"Girl, that man is so far off the single radar. You see that young looking chick with the other women," she replies.

"She's very pretty, but she looks young enough to still be in high school" I state.

"She is. Her name is Selena and she has his nose open so wide that you can walk past him naked and he wouldn't notice you," she state.

"Aren't you the one that said any man is fair game?" I question.

"There are a few rare exceptions that a woman has her game so tight that her man never strays away. From what I have seen that's one. By the way thanks," she tells.

"Thanks for what?" I ask.

"Your fake smile actually seems real," she whispers before they came back with our drinks.

We have great seats. They are dead center in the second row. Of course we sit right behind Robert and his girlfriend. I had to watch the two of them cuddle and kiss all night. That is on fine ass man.

Why does Jason keep trying to hold my hand like we are on a real date? I wish he stop the small talk, I would like to hear the performances. My trip to the bathroom is the most annoy thing. Instead of moving his feet so I can walk by he stands up forcing my body to rub up against his. As much as I enjoy Kem I'm glad to see this night coming to an end.

"Let's grab something to eat," Brittany suggest on the way home.

"What would you like Baby" Shannon ask.

"Nothing fancy. Fifth Avenue's is up the street," she suggests.

"Do you all mind stopping to get something to eat?" Shannon asks.

"Sounds good," Jason reply.

"It will be fine," I reluctantly reply knowing I want this date to end.

As I sit there listening to the three of them talk two familiar faces walk through the door. It's Darrell and one of his frat brothers. What else can go wrong tonight! Damn, his ass might notice me. Now, I'm going to have to interact with this Jason guy. Maybe that motherfucker will get the hint that I have moved on.

I've been acting nice for the last hour and that motherfucker hasn't noticed me. Guess I have to make my presence known.

"Do you play pool?" I ask Jason.

"Yes, do you?" he reply.

"No, but I would like to learn," I suggest.

"I'll be right back. Let me pay for a table and get the pool balls," he replies.

"There's no way Darrell will be able to miss seeing me," I thought to myself.

"It appears Spring is warming up to my man," Shannon mention to Brittany as they walk away.

"Let's keep our fingers crossed," Brittany replies.

"Have you ever held a pool stick?" Jason asks handing me a pool stick.

"I have never been around a pool table," I admit.

"Let me explain the game to you," he rambles on.

Across the room Spring attracts someone's attention.

"Man is that chick over there with the banging body your old girl from school," Darrell's friend points out.

"It is, but who the hell is she with!" Darrel replies turning around to get a better look.

"Damn, she still is fine," his friend state.

"I'll be right back," he says.

Jason places his hand on mine to show me the proper position of my fingers. He position behind me molding his body to mine as he leans me forward. He then wraps his hand around my hand that was holding the pool stick.

"Just relax and allow your movement to flow with my guidance," Jason instructs.

"So, I hit the white ball with enough force to hit at least one ball into a pocket," I comment.

"Yes. Damn you smell good," he states.

"Thanks. Pool doesn't seem too hard," I reply.

"It's not. Once you find the rhythm of your stroke," he responds.

"Excuse me, Spring can I have a moment of your time?" Darrell asks interrupting the pool game.

"Like I explained the last time, we have nothing to discuss," I respond.

"Baby, I'm sorry about that," Darrell apologizes.

"I'm not your baby. You walked out of my life once and you need to stay out," I respond.

"But Spring," Darrel reply.

"Babe," Jason said referring to Spring.

"Babe," Darrell surprisingly repeats.

"Do you know this joker?" Jason asks.

"He's part of my past," I reply.

"You need to watch who you're calling a joker," Darrell angrily growl.

"I'm not asking. I'm demanding that you respect my lady's wishes and leave her the fuck alone," Jason demand.

"This is between Spring and I," Darrel claims.

"I became involved the moment you came over interrupting our game!" Jason informs.

"Is there a problem over here," the manager asks stepping between Darrell and Jason.

"No. I'm leaving," Darrell state.

"Are you ok?" Jason asks.

"Yes. Thanks for having my back," I acknowledge giving him a hug and light kiss.

"Do you want to finish the game?"Jason asks.

"Think I had enough," I reply.

"Back so soon," Shannon comment when they return to the table.

"Where is the lady's bathroom?" I ask.

"It's over there. I'll come with you," Brittany responds.

"Did you see that motherfucker that walk up on us at the pool table," Jason asks Shannon.

"No. What the hell happened?" Shannon respond with a question

"I'm assuming it was Spring's old boyfriend. I can't believe she lost her virginity to that ugly motherfucker," he replies.

"How did she react?" Shannon asks.

"She demanded for him to leave her alone and I backed her up. He better be lucky management stepped between us," he explains.

"Where is he?" Shannon asks.

"He's that ugly one in the Polo shirt," he answers pointing his finger at Darrell and making sure he sees.

"You two are hitting it off well," Brittany comments while we were in the little lady's room.

"That mother fucker Darrell is here. He walked up to our pool table and Jason backed him off me," I explain.

"Damn, I missed that," she responds.

"Girl, I need to be broken off tonight," I admit.

"I was wondering how long you were going to wait to get you some dick. I just wasn't expecting it to be tonight," Brittany replies.

"After seeing Darrell my shit is horny. I'm pretty sure that Jason will not have problem hosing me down," I laugh.

"You're stupid," Brittany says as we laugh on our way back to the table.

"I'm ready to call it a night," Brittany mentions as she standing behind Shannon's chair rubbing on his chest.

"Me too," Shannon agrees throwing more than enough cash to cover the bill and a phat tip.

Jason grabs me around the waist and proudly escorts me out of the bar. I cut my eyes at Darrell follow by a quick flip of my middle finger as we pass by his table.

It's a quite ride home. It's a quiet ride home. My head is laying on Jason's shoulder as we hold hands on the ride home. Jason is a lucky man tonight I have a whole lot of pinned up sexual frustration to release. After seeing that bitch ass Darrell makes what to me want to fix the tension. Fucking the shit out of Jason is my way of getting back at Darrell's ass.

Shannon offers Jason his keys in case he chooses to leave. Brittany and Shannon retire to her bedroom while Jason and I relax in front of the big flat screen TV in the entertainment room. He's sitting on the couch indulging me in complements.

"I'm assuming that guy back at the bar was your old boyfriend! You are a very beautiful woman and I understand why that joker wants you back," Jason comment.

"Yes, he was. There are some parts to my past that should stay in the past and he is one," I answer.

"His loss is defiantly my gain," he replies.

"Is talking all you have planned on doing tonight?" I ask starring him in the eyes.

"Not unless you have something else in mind," he responds scanning me up and down.

I proceed to straddle him sitting on his lap. "I hate to be bold about this. It's been over eight months, since I have had any sexual contact," I said as I was unbuttoning my sweater.

"Damn baby," he said as his eyes widen at the sight of my big breast in a red lacy bra.

"The way you took control of that situation impressed the hell out of me and made me hot," I lied knowing that me seeing Darrell is the only reason why I'm sitting on his lap right now.

"You are the finest woman I have ever seen," Jason said with the look of someone trying to hold back drool.

"Do you have a condom?" I ask.

"Yes, I do," he answers while scrambling in his pants pocket.

I engage him in a deep tongue kiss, while he holds on to my breast. I let him take turns sucking on my breast. I rotate my pelvis over his dick to speed up his erection.

It's a beautiful sight watching her standing there stripping off the remaining of her clothes. She took everything off but her jewelry. I rush to undress and roll my condom on.

Without any words between us I straddle him allowing my wet hot pussy to descend on his fully erected dick. I intertwine my fingers with his and lean back to ride his dick.

"Ohhhhhh," I moan as my body began releasing my pinned up sexual tension.

"Ohhhhhhh, this is some good pussy," he moans back.

He lowers my back onto the oversized ottoman that sits in front of the couch. He got on his knees. I wrap my legs around his back. He squeezes my breast while fucking me good.

"Ohhhh Spring," he moans.

"Ohhhh, ohhhh, ohhhh, ohhhhhhhhh," I moan as my legs began to shake as my body prepares to cum.

"Ohhhhhhhhhh," he moan again as he prepare to cum.

"Do you have another condom?" I ask.

"I have a couple," he replies.

"Grab your clothes we can finish this in my bedroom," I state while leading him upstairs for round two.

Chapter 15

"What the hell did I do last night," I thought to myself as I stare at the naked sleeping man in my bed. "It is what it is. It feels good using someone to numb the heartache," I admit to myself as I threw on something and head downstairs to make a cup of coffee.

I'm sitting on the living room couch enjoying my caramel vanilla cream coffee when I notice Darrell's car pulling up.

"What the hell are you doing here?" a harshly ask opening the front door.

"Baby, I understand it was me that fucked up our relationship. If you give me a chance I can make it up to you. We can work through it," Darrell pleads.

"There's nothing you can do to fix this situation. Technically you lied every time you claim to love me," I state.

"I never lied about that. I truly loved you and I'm still in love with you," he replies.

"You didn't love me. I was nothing more than your campus piece of ass," I state.

"You were the one that I really wanted to build a future with. I thought I was doing right for a baby that turned out not to be mine," he try explaining.

"I have moved on," I respond.

"Not with that thug from last night!" he slurs.

"Yes," I sharply reply.

"You deserve better than him. He doesn't appear to be your type," he suggests.

"He wasn't my type until last night!" I claim.

"What is that suppose to mean?" he ask.

"Last night was the first time I have given another man a moment of my time, since being dumped by email. I had one brief moment of missing you. So, I closed my eyes and imagined he was you that I was kissing. That quickly turned into anger. So, I released all my pinned up sexual frustration on him several times last night. I had that boy screaming my name," I disclose with a grin on my face.

"Please give me a chance. I won't judge you for your indiscretion," he replies.

"Judge my indiscretion! You must be out of your damn mind," I angrily respond.

Jason realizes Spring is not lying next to him so he slid on his boxers and pants before heading towards the muffled voices. He descends down the stairs at the moment that Darrell is declaring his love for Spring.

"Spring I love you," Darrell admits.

"I thought I made myself perfectly clear last night. I don't want anything to do with you," I reply.

"But Spring," he said.

"Let me repeat myself. I have moved on and you need to do the same," I respond.

"You need to get the fuck on," Jason interjects after hearing only the end of their conversation.

"Partner this has nothing to do with you," Darrell snaps after noticing he just rolled out of Spring's bed.

"First, I'm not your motherfucking partner and for two like she said she has moved on and you need to do the same," Jason threaten while pushing Darrell off the porch.

"You need to keep your hands to yourself," Darrell order.

"What?" Jason said while charging at him like a raging bull.

"Stop," I yell jumping in the middle to break up the fight.

"Darrell you need to get the fuck on," I demand while holding Jason back.

"You're going to choose that punk over me?" Darrell questions.

"For the last time. I have moved on and you need to leave me the hell alone," I instruct.

"Yeah right," Jason add holding his arm up and using his hand's thumb and first finger to symbolize a gun.

I quickly kiss Jason to shut his ass up and to make Darrell jealous.

"You will regret your discussion one day," Darrell yells out as he pulls off.

"Are you ok?" Jason proudly asks believing Spring considers him as her man.

"Let's go in the house," I nonchalantly request.

Later that day Brittany and I sit around talking about this morning and last night events.

"Shannon called after he dropped Jason off and he said the man could not stop talking about you. He is actually a nice guy," she says.

"I'm not ready for a relationship," I state.

"It wouldn't hurt you to let someone be nice to you. If you keep laying it on him like you did last night he will be putty in your hands," she inform.

"That don't mean shit to me," I reply.

"You're always bitching about your student loans. He'll pay your tuition and probably pay off you outstanding student loans," she responds.

"Umm, I have nothing to lose and I have to admit he was a great fuck. Hell, I might as well. As long as there is no drama with other women," I note.

"I know for sure that Jason doesn't have any permanent bitches or babies hiding in the background," she state.

"Admit it, you set me up? You could have handled them women last night?" I question.

"Yeah, I thought you needed a push. I just wasn't expecting you to dusk off your cobwebs that soon," she respond.

"Hell, it would not have happen if it wasn't for me running into Darrell. It was amusing seeing Jason check his ass for the second time this morning," I disclose.

"I still don't believe we slept through that shit this morning," Brittany mentions.

Chapter 16

"Damn, for the last few weeks every time I want to hangout you got your head in a book. Are you trying to blow me off?" Jason complains.

"No, I feel out of place around your friends," I claim.

"You shouldn't. They are just ordinary people," he state.

"I'm not talking about the men. Their women are always so glamorous," I admit.

"That's because they spend all their free time getting their hair and nails done, while you spend all your free time in your books," he reply.

"I would pamper myself from time to time if I wasn't paying for grad school," I respond.

"You still need to treat yourself," he mention.

"I will after I graduation," I inform.

"Ok, let me handle this. Tomorrow I'm going to take you by my sister's beauty salon," he state.

"Since, that sounds like a long day event I'm giving you a pass to hang out with your boys tonight so I can knock out my homework," I insist.

"Do you mind me coming back later?" he asks.

"Not at all," I reply knowing I enjoy the extra workout.

Chapter 17

Jason stops by his sister's beauty salon on 7 Mile off Schaefer in Detroit.

"I need a big favor from you," Jason request as he walk up to his sister's chair.

"Ok, what's the big favor?" Fran answers.

"I'm going to bring my girlfriend up here tomorrow. I want her to receive the works with your best employees, but you are the only one I want to touch her hair and eyebrows," he demands.

"You're scared your old girl might say something!" she jokes.

"Not really. I believe she would do a shitty job just to get back at my ass," he claims.

"You know this is going to cost. So make sure she has enough money," she state.

"I will be paying the bill when I pick her up," he replies.

"You're paying her bill and providing the transportation. What's really going on?" she question.

"I think mom would approve of this one," he mentions.

"You plan to introduce her to mama?" she asks.

"Yes," he replies.

"How long have you been dating her?" she asks.

"She was my date at the Kem concert," he responds.

"You go through women so fast I stop noticing them. You know I'm going to put her through my fifty questions, because something must be wrong with her," she jokingly comments.

"Why something has to be wrong with her?" he question.

"Don't get me wrong I love you, but you're a man slut!" she state.

"A leopard can always change his spots," he state.

"Your spots are not the only problem. I have seen your taste in women and it's frightening," she laughs.

"Trying something different," he state.

"Ok, what's the punch line?" she jokes.

"There is no punch line. She's beautiful and intelligent," he replies.

"You can bring her in tomorrow. I want to check her out!" she responds.

Chapter 18

Jason proudly escorts me into the salon.

"This is my sister Fran. This is my girlfriend Spring," Jason introduces.

"You can take her to my booth. I'll be there in a minute," Fran instructs as she carefully scan Spring for any physical defects. "Ok, the girl doesn't appear to have Down syndrome, isn't retarded, or has any physical handicaps so she must be an airhead or a hoe. Those are the only excuses I can see why someone that beautiful would be dating my brother," she thought to herself.

I remember seeing his sister at the concert. She seems to be a good ten years older than Jason. You can tell they are related. They have the same facial features. The only difference is she has a mole in the center of her right cheek. Whatever she has on under her smock has to be sharp to go with her Gucci riding boots.

"So Spring, how did you meet my brother?" Fran ask while washing my hair.

"On a blind date for the Kem concert," I admit.

"Why would you need to be setup on a blind date?" she ask being intrigue

"My girl thought it was time for me to jump back into the dating scene," I reply.

"It doesn't appear that you would have a problem finding a date," she state

"After the break up with my last boyfriend, dating was not on my to do list," I state.

"How long did you all date?" she asks.

"We dated all through college," I blurt out.

"I take it you have a college degree!" she quiz.

"Yes, in finance," I respond.

"What are your plans now that you are out of college?" she asks.

"I'm working at a financial firm downtown, while working on a master's degree at Wayne State. I plan to get my doctoral degree before my 27th birthday," I inform.

"Why so many degrees?" she question.

"My goal is to become the youngest female CFO at the firm," I acknowledge.

"Ok, you're beautiful, smart, and seem to have a level head. What do you see in my brother?" she asks being puzzled that she is nothing like the other chicks her brother usually messes around with.

"He is really sweet and caring," I answer thinking of something nice to say about him.

"He's sweet and caring! On that note I'm going to need you to sit under the hair dryer for an hour," she commands while escorting her to a dryer.

Fran goes back to her booth mystified. "My brother never deals with woman that has a brain and beauty. They have a brain and butt ugly or pretty and an airhead or whore. I think he is biting off more than he can chew with this one. For his sake I hope it works out," she silently thinks to herself until someone loudly calling her name from across the room breaks her thoughts.

"Fran, come here for a minute," a guy sitting in one of the barber chairs yell out.

"What is it Lamont," she ask walking up to him.

"Who is that fine ass chick in your chair?" he question.

"That's my little brother's girlfriend. She's off limits to you," she responds.

"We'll see about that," he claims.

"Don't make me have my man band you from the shop," she state.

"Girl, Dean is not going to do anything," he replies.

"Didn't you just get your hair cut the other day?" she remark.

"I have to look fresh. Never know who I might meet," he claims winking his right eye.

"You're such a man slut," she replies.

"I'm no different than any hair salon," he responds.

"How could that possible be?" she ask.

"I provide a service that all women need," he state grabbing his crouch.

"You're stupid. Remember leave that one in my chair alone," she sternly demand.

I spent the entire afternoon getting, a pedicure, a manicure, a facial, and my hair styled. Jason walks into the salon as his sister is finishing up with my hair.

When she spun me around I'm stunned at my reflection in the mirror. I'm identical to pictures of my mother when she in the Miss Michigan Beauty Pageant. If I didn't know any better I would have thought I was looking at the cover of a magazine.

"You did an amazing job. So what do you think about Spring?" Jason questions her as he pulls her over to the side.

"She's extremely pretty and highly intelligent, but I think she might be out your league," she state.

"What do you mean, out of my league?" he questions.

"A woman like that will become bored with you once she gets her career together," she mentions.

"She's not like that!" he reply.

"Be careful, that's all I have to say," she states.

"Don't worry, I got this," he reply while proudly noticing that every man in the shop is eyeing Spring.

"We need to go to the mall and find you something extremely sexy and hit the club tonight," he suggests.

"A new outfit is not in my budget. I should be able to find something at home," I mention.

"Don't worry I got this. All you have to do is look drop dead gorgeous, which isn't hard for you," he state.

"Thanks to your sister I can manage that," I reply. "Brittany is right about men throwing their money at a beautiful woman. I didn't realize how easy it was. I guess it want hurt letting him spend his money on me," I think to myself.

Chapter 19

I can't believe a whole year has passed. I should be finishing up with grad school next year and ready to spread my wings further up the corporate ladder. Soon Brittany will have Marcus out her live and I can kick Jason to the curb after he pays off my last semester of school.

"Like always he comes bearing gifts," I said out loud as I notice him pulling out a big white box adorn with an equally large red bow.

Time to play make believe. I need to put on my fake girlfriend game face and enjoy tonight's couple festivities with him and his people.

"What do you have there?" I ask welcoming him in the house.

"Just open the box!" he reply holding it out.

"I love you," I mistakenly blurts out, while pulling a full length mink coat out the box.

"I love you too," he replies helping me put the coat on.

"Ohhhh, shit I meant to say I love the mink," I think to myself as I slip into the coat. "Why, such an elaborate gift? Christmas is still a month away," I ask.

"My woman shouldn't go out wearing her girl's mink coat," he claims.

"You are a good man," I lie while embracing him in a hug.

"The price of being in love," he replies before engaging me in a kiss.

"I think we need to go before you start something," I suggest.

"Your right," he agrees.

It looks as if almost everyone is pulling up at the same time to valet parking in the back of the General Motors building. We proceed upstairs to Seldom Blues which is a jazz supper club. The elegant contemporary style of the restaurant is enhanced with a fabulous view of the Detroit River and Windsor, Canada as the backdrop.

Luckily we had reservations, because the place is packed and the wait to seat a party of eighteen would have taken all night. I silently wait hoping that Brittany and Shannon show up soon as the group talks amongst each other.

"Hello Spring, Jason told me you're in graduate school," Selena said starting a conversation as she walks up.

"Yes. I'm working on my masters in finance," I respond being surprise that someone in the group notice my presence.

"I'm planning to start college right after graduation. One of these days I would like to talk with you about the transition from high school to college," she rambles on.

"That sounds fine," I state.

"Thanks," she replies.

"That was awkward. She seems to be really nice, but that's not going to stop me from lusting over her man," I laugh to myself as we are escorted to the table.

Brittany and Shannon are being escorted to the table just as Jason's sister Fran and her man Dean walks in.

During dinner the other woman actually includes me in their conversations. I wonder are they being nice to me because Jason and I have been together for a while, the fact that Fran accepts me as her brother's woman, or that Selena seems to be friendly with me. After several bottles of expensive wine and rounds of alcohol drinks they even seem to include Brittany in their conversation.

It's obvious his boys Dean, Lamont, Gator, and Robert are making more money than him. They seem to be bigger payouts than Jason. Don't get me wrong he's making good money in the street, just not as much them. I would get more money if I was fucking one of the other guys?

Dean seems a little too laid back for me. Him and his girl acts like an old married couple. He probably thinks sitting in front of the television is an exciting evening. I wouldn't be surprised if they only fuck once a week.

I can tell his boy Lamont wants me. He's always staring me down like I'm naked, goes out of his way to talk to me, and always trying to rub up against me regardless if he's with a date or not. His eyes almost popped out his head when Jason helped me out my mink at coat check. I do have on a red low cut wrap around dress that's hugging every curve perfectly. The fact that he flirts with me in front of his dates validates he's a dog.

Gator seems a little off in a scary sort of way. Besides, his girl appears to be a force to be reckoned with. I can see her jumping out of bushes, playing on my phone, and talking trash about me on the social networks. I don't need the drama.

Now Robert is fine as hell. I would entertain fucking around with him. The only problem is that he doesn't seem to acknowledge that I existence. When Selena's around it seems that no one else exists in his world.

Besides, if I did some shit and fuck around with one of them it I would definitely cause problems within their street family. Most of all it could cause tension between Brittany and I. It's not worth losing my friendship with her.

Let me throw the thoughts out my mind and concentrate on enjoying myself. Jason is not that bad. At least he's a good fuck that I can count on several times a week and sometimes several times a day. I don't have to worry about waking up to find him standing over me at night like a crazy man. In his world I am the finest woman around and he will do damn near anything to please me.

"I'll be back," I whisper to Jason as I notice Brittany heading to the lady's bathroom. I caught a glimpse of Lamont watching as Jason stare down my top as I lean in to whisper in his ear.

"I heard ole boy bought you a mink coat," Brittany mentions.

"Girl, I made the biggest mistake," I said.

"What's the problem?" she asks.

"When I open the box I blurted out I love you," I reveal.

"Shannon told me that Jason is all in love with you. So, I know he was excited to know you feel the same," she responds.

"I was talking about the coat and not him," I share.

"Did you tell him that?" she questions.

"He blurted out his love for me before I could say anything. Like a punk I didn't say anything," I reply.

"Look at it this way. You will be able to get a lot more out if he thinks you love him," she informs.

"Hell, I need a new ride," I suggest.

"Play your cards right, you might be driving a new car very soon," she state.

"That's not a bad goal to work towards and I think I will start working on it tonight," I said.

When I made it back to the table I gave him a sweet enduring kiss on the cheek.

"What was that for?" he whisper.

"Just because," I whisper back.

"Thanks," he replies kissing me back.

The remaining of the evening I upped my game of being the committed girlfriend. I treat him like a king. I even act to like his friends' fake ass women.

I'm not sure what our bill came up to, but each man seems to lay three to four hundred dollars on the table. As we all stands at coat check the clerk hand one mink coat after another. I can tell Lamont's date feel out of place when they hands him her wool coat.

"You really have no idea what this Thursday is?" Jason asks as we wait for valet to bring his truck around.

"Am I missing something here?" I answer with a question.

"I know you claim to hate holidays, but I'm surprised you forgot. Last year we went on our first date," he responds.

"Sorry, my bad. I didn't realize it's been a year. Is that the reason you gave me the mink coat?" I question.

"Some what!" he replies.

"I feel so bad that I forgot and don't have anything for you," I respond acting concerned.

"You can make it up to me several times tonight," he suggests.

"You're on," I agree knowing the bedroom is one place I truly enjoy his companionship.

Damn, it has been a year since that asshole Darrell tried to weasels his ass back into my live. If it wasn't for that night I probably would have given in and took him back.

Looking back Darrell treated me as a prize possession and Jason treats me as the grand prize.   Darrell was satisfied with the simple things in life, but Jason always likes to do things big and flashy. Clearly my life isn't meant to be simple.

"What are you thinking about?" Jason question

"I still can't believe it's been a year," I respond leaning a little closer.

"Is that a good thing or a bad thing?" he asks.

"It's the first time in my life I had a drama free year. So, I can honestly say it's a good thing," I reply grabbing hold of his free hand.

"Hope I contribution a little to that!" he respond.

"Actually you made a big contribution to last year being good for me," I state knowing he is the main reason for me getting rid of Darrel.

"I'm aimed to please," he mentions.

"I will hold you to that," I admit realizing the coat is a sign of his money being mine.

I sit back evaluating my situation. I don't have to be in love to be in a relationship. I have good dick on call, he enjoys buying me expensive gifts, and he financial supports all my entertainment expenses, while worshiping the ground I walk on. All I have to do is allow him to be in my presence. Best of all his pockets are paying for my college tuition, books, and all my daily living expenses, which allow me to bank my pay checks. I'm ok with a relationship of convenience. I can have all the benefits of a relationship without having any real emotional ties.

Chapter 20

Every time he drinks too much we end up at his little house on the upper west side of Detroit. I only call it little because it's less than half the size of Brittany's house. It's all he needs. At least the area is still stable. It also helps having several retired cops as neighbors.

It's a modest three bedroom 1 ½ bathroom ranch. The living room/dining room consist of nothing but two large couches, a loveseat, and an entertainment center to house his 75 inch flat screen television, cable box, and speakers. If it wasn't for the mixed match dishes and cups the kitchen would be completely bare. The two spare bedrooms are smaller than my college dorm room. His master bedroom is not much bigger and poorly decorated. All he has is a king size bed that sits high off the floor and a 50 inch flat screen television mounted to the wall. There's not one sign of a woman's touch in the entire house.

Since, his block is dead silence I'm going to treat him to a special gift. The moment he parks his truck it's on. I climb into the driver's seat engaging him in a deep tongue kiss after he cuts the truck off.

It doesn't take much for Spring to turn me on. Let me adjust my seat as far back as it will go. Despite the fact that she's straddled over me, I'm still able to unfasten my pants and pull them down far enough to free my throbbing dick.

I slid the crotch of my thongs over to insert his partially erect dick into my wet pussy. I lean my back against the steering wheel to watch the expression on his face as his dick swell to a full erection as I grind on it.

As, I stare at her beautiful face the only thing I can think about is how lucky I am. She is the total package. One of the finest lady's in the street and my personal freak.

"OOOhhhhhh," he moans.

I tighten my pussy muscle as my strokes sped up. This trick always makes him cum faster. All he needs is a five minute teaser before the main attraction.

"I may not have remembered our one year mile stone, but I do appreciate everything you have done for me," I share.

"That was a hell of a way to thank a nigga!" he admits with a smile on his face.

"I'm not done thanking you yet," I state as I climb out his truck and like a well-trained puppy he's a few steps behind.

After closing the front door I take off my mink coat throwing it across the loveseat. I stand in the middle of his living room untying my dress allowing it to slide to the floor.

Spring is smoking hot. Damn my money is well spent I thinking as she stands in a sexy black bra and thong set wearing a pair of red leather six inch platform thigh high boots.

His clothes seem to fly off as he rushes towards me. The next thing I know he picks me off my feet carrying me to his bedroom. He lays me across his bed and quickly slid my thongs down my legs.

"Do you need me to take off my boots," I question.

"Not at all, but I would like for you to turn on your stomach," he request.

The second she rolls on her stomach I pull her legs off the bed placing them on the floor. Just the thrill of fucking her instantly makes my dick hard. I hold on to her ass with one hand as I used the other hand to guide my dick for backdoor entrance into her hot wet pussy.

"Ooooohhhh, that feels good," I scream out in sheer pleasure.

"Whose pussy is this?" he question.

"This is Jason's pussy," I state.

"This dick love being all up in your hot wet pussy," he claims.

"I want every inch of your dick inside of my pussy," I request.

"Baby, I plan to give you every inch," he replies while stroking slowly.

The pace of his strokes deepens my sexual pleasure. It feels so good that I can't help myself from joining in with a slow gyrating thrusting of my hips to the rhythm of his strokes. We go on like this for a good long time. My legs begin shaking uncontrollable as my body explodes with excitement.

I pull out and lift her onto the bed. She rolls on her back. As she scoots up the bed I climb in between her legs forcing them to hang over my shoulders. I'm making sure her legs stay drape over my shoulders as my dick works its way back into her wet pussy. I watch as she grasp for air at each deep stroke of my dick.

His dick is extraordinary good tonight. Did it have anything to do with those three words I made a mistake and said? There is one way of finding out.

"I love you," I yell out when his strokes sped up.

"I love you too," he replies slowing his strokes.

Our bodies are dripping with sweat. I lay one of her legs on the bed as the other remains over my shoulder. I roll us onto one side and continue fucking her.

The extra sexual simulation of him sucking on my breast is driving my body crazy. I'm trying my best to hold back from releasing an orgasm, but I cannot help myself.

"Ooooooohhhh." I loudly moan as my entire body begins shaking.

"Yaaaaahhhhhhhhhhhhhhhhhhhh shit," he moans out while holding me tightly wrapped in his arms.

"That was quick but amazing." I admit.

"It could be like this every night if you move in," he suggests.

"Where did that come from?" I question.

"I love you and you love me. It only makes sense," he state.

"I can't move out of Brittany's house," I respond.

"Why not?" he asks.

"It's just not the right time," I reply.

"What do you mean not the right time?" he asks.

"I made a promise to Brittany that I wouldn't move out until her situation is straighten out," I explain.

"Things change," he state.

"She was there when my father took my mother's live. She took me in with no hesitation when my word was all I had to offer. Honoring my word is the least I can do to show my gratuity," I elaborate.

"I can understand your loyalty, but I'm not giving up," he informs.

"Thanks for understanding," I reply engaging him in a kiss. "Brittany is right about this man being head over heels for me. That's good for me and bad for his bank roll," I think to myself.

Chapter 21

I really fucked up when those three words slipped out. Now he wants to introduce me to his entire family at his grandmother's Thanksgiving dinner today. I wouldn't be going if it wasn't for me wanting a new car.

On the bright side my girl Carrie will be in town tomorrow for a marketing conference. If, I can drag Yolanda from her new man we can have an unofficial girl's night out this Friday. I will need a night to unwind after spending Thanksgiving with Jason's family.

We pull up to a cute colonel brick house on the Westside of Detroit. I can tell from the huge picture window they are having a big family gathering for Thanksgiving dinner. The moment I walk through the front door my heart begins to race. I feel like all eyes are on me. Not sure if it's because the holidays bring up such hurtful memories from my past or his grandmother's statement.

"Grandma this beautiful lady is,' Jason try introducing.

"This has to be Spring. Your mother told me she was pretty. She must be special for my favorite grandson to bring her around. Come over here and give me a hug," she loudly announces while holding her arms out.

"It's nice to finally meet you," I reply hugging her while noticing his other relatives rushing towards the front hallway.

Everyone starts introducing themselves, hugging me, and asking a million questions. His sister Fran and her man Dean are talking to me like we are actually friends. I must be the main attraction. It wouldn't be that bad if everyone stop trying to provoke conversations with me and asking us to pose together for pictures.

Every time his uncles or male cousins complement his taste in women I want to slap that stupid grin he makes off his face. No telling what he has told them about our relationship. Oops, I meant my fake relationship. I must keep this plastic smile on my face and continue acting like the happy girlfriend.

The goal of getting a new car is an excellent reason to put up with his family's holiday tradition. The remaining of the evening I will make sure he thinks he's the man. It may take for me to occasional touch him affectionately and passionately respond to his light kisses.

Chapter 22

"Are you sure I'm not inconveniencing you? We can drive my rental car" Carrie suggest as I pick her up from her hotel.

"Not at all, I prefer driving his truck," I admit.

"Will I get the chance to meet this Jason guy Yolanda seems to disapprove of?" she asks.

"Yea, when I switch vehicles with him," I reply.

"Is it that serious between the two of you?" she question.

"It may be for him, but not for me. He's a good piece of dick that serves a financial purpose," I admit.

"He couldn't be all that bad if he's letting you drive his vehicle," she suggests.

"I only requested the switch to speed up the process of him buying me a new car," I mention.

"That's a statement I expect to hear from your girl Brittany," she comment.

"A lot of Brittany's crazy ass theories about men didn't make sense until after Darrell showed his ass," I state.

"That's no reason to dog the man out," she responds.

"I'm sure he has dogged out his fair share of women," I suggest.

"That's still not a good excuse for you to mistreat the man because of the way Darrell did you," she replies.

"Hold that thought!" I state as we pull up to Jason's house.

"Hey baby, this is my girl Carrie," I say introducing her. "Thanks for letting me drive your truck tonight," I mention while handing over my car keys and taking hold for his truck keys.

"It's nice to finally meet you, Jason," Carrie responds to acknowledge his presences.

"Good meeting you too," he replies. "Damn you look good. I filled the tank up and here's some extra cash. Have a good time. I'm meeting up with the fellows tonight so I will catch up with you tomorrow," he says.

"Thanks," I reply giving him a hug and kiss.

"That was some shit back there," Carrie comment as we pull off.

"What are you talking about?" I question.

"You didn't have the decency to properly introduce the man and he didn't even notice," she state.

"That's why I treat him the way a do," I mention.

"What happen to my girl Spring?" she ask.

"She wised up. Hope you don't have a problem with the improved Spring," I state.

"Nay, she might be a lot more fun than that love sick puppy. Just surprised at the type of man you're dating," she respond.

"I'm not looking to make this a long term thing, but it works for now," I admit.

"I understand that," she replies.

"I'll be glad when Yolanda sees that I'm not looking to make him my husband. All I need is a good piece of dick that's happy spending every dime on me," I joke.

"Talking about Yolanda are you picking her up?" she ask.

"Her man is dropping her off later. They have choir practice or something," I reply.

"Have you met her new man?" she asks.

"You know I don't do the church thing and they seem to spend a lot of time there. She wants us to double date, but I can't image him and Jason having anything in common. Besides I don't want Jason to get any more notions that I'm taking this fake relationship to another level," I reply.

"Thought we were heading downtown to your old spot?" she question.

"Nay, I figured we hit this new club. The food is pretty good and they have a VIP sections," I reply.

"Look at that line. Shit the parking lot is full and valet parking is closed," she complains.

"Girl, I got this," I inform as I stop in front of the club and a security guard come running up to the driver's side window.

"Hey, Spring no Jason tonight?" the security guard question after I roll down the window.

"No. It's a girls' night out," I respond.

"Cool. Let me clear the crowd so you can park," he instructs.

"They are actually moving the people out the way so you can park near the entrance," she says being amazed.

"One of Jason's boy's owns the club and this is his designated parking spot. Don't touch the door handle when I cut the truck off. It's VIP all night long," I drill.

Two security guards run up to open both ours doors. I enjoy watching the facial expressions on all the busters standing in line as I step out of the truck in my mink coat walking to the head of the line.

"Good evening Spring and who is the lovely lady with you?" the man at the front door asks while greeting me with a hug.

"This is my college sister Carrie. Carrie this is Omar the owner of the club," I introduce.

"Nice to meet you Ms. Carrie," he acknowledges as he escorts us in.

"There is one more joining us tonight. Can you have someone escort her up to our usually VIP section," I request.

"Sure. Brittany and a few of her friends are already up there," he informs.

Chapter 23

"Hey Jason, I thought Robert was the only love sick nigga. Now your ass is driving Spring's broke down car," Lamont mention.

"Jealously is not a good look on you," I respond.

"Hey your girl may be fine, but a hoe is a hoe," he replies.

"I know for sure that my girl has only been with one other man. Bet you can't say the same thing for the tricks you mess around with," I threw back at him.

"Man you better watch out. Someone might creep in if you're ever caught slipping," he insist.

"I'm not worried about my game," I admit with confidence that my relationship is rock solid.

"Gentlemen, you all can finish that conversation after we wrap up this meeting," Gator orders.

"We need to discuss New Year's. For those that are going to the meeting in LA. Corey and I decided everyone must be in Las Vegas by the 29th. We are driving to LA for the meeting on the 30th. I also, decided to make this a mini vacation with our women," Dean informs the group.

"In Lamont's case just a mini vacation with a random hoe," Robert jokes.

"Everyone that's going need to book a room at my favorite hotel, the Bellagio," Dean insists.

"What about our girls while we're in LA," Shannon asks.

"We're driving back right after the meeting. Besides, I thought it would be a perfect day for them to spend shopping. Robert you should be ok for a couple of days, while we are gone," Dean instructs.

"Robert. You should have fallen in love with someone old enough to travel without needing her father's permission," Lamont tease.

"Fuck you. You jealous motherfucker," Robert reply.

Chapter 24

When we get to our VIP section three of Brittany girls are up here, but no Brittany. Apparently she's out dancing. I introduce everyone to Carrie. From the looks on Brittany's friends' faces I could tell they're not to please that my girl is white, but who gives a fuck what they think. Her girl Cherry that used to fuck around with Jason is going to hate on me any way.

"That's a beautiful sheer top. Isn't it a little risky for you?" Cherry questions.

"I thought the bra was too cute and expensive to hide," I reply.

"Are those knock off boots?" she ask.

"No, my man brought them and this purse from the Michael Kors' store at Somerset Mall," I brag.

"That's sweet he buys you a few trinkets, but you're still driving that shitty ass car," she laugh.

"If I gave me this mink coat for the anniversary of our first date, just think of what I will get for the anniversary of our first fuck," I insultingly slang back.

"Now, now girls let's play nice," Brittany order as she enter the VIP section.

"She was admiring Jason's taste," I state.

"Hey, Brittany," Carrie greets trying to changing the subject.

"Are you staying at the house this weekend?" Brittany asks while giving her a big hug.

"No, I'm in for a conference and the company picking up my hotel bill," Carrie answer.

"We will be downstairs where the air is not so foul," Cherry announces as her and the other women get up to leave.

"It was nice seeing you again," I reply while waving bye.

"Did he switch vehicles with you?" Brittany asks.

"He did," I answer.

"Do you know what to do in order to seal the deal?" Brittany asks.

"I thought letting him see the condition of my car is all I need to do," I mention.

"You need to give the man a blow job," Brittany suggest.

"Yuck. Put his dick in my mouth," I state with my face twisted up.

"Yes, suck his dick," Brittany insists.

"That's nasty," I claim.

"You mean all the fucking you and Darrell did, you never sucked his dick?" Carrie questions.

"Hell nay. You sucked a dick before?" I question.

"It's not that bad once you get past the gagging phase," Carrie mentions.

"Once you get your technique together it's like enjoying a sucker or popsicle," Brittany suggests.

"It's still gross," I reply.

"I was extremely drunk my first time," Carrie admit.

"How did you remember sucking a dick if you were drunk," I ask.

"It was like an out of body experience and the next morning the fool claim to be in love," Carrie explains.

"You have to make the first move before he mention the condition of your car. If you suck a little dick, tell him how much he means to you, and say, I love you like you mean it, you will be able to pick the make and color of your car," Brittany instructs.

"I would be lying to him," I disclose.

"You've been doing a damn good job of fooling him this long. If you get enough alcohol in you and pretend you're acting out a love scene from your favorite movie it should help," Brittany recommends.

"I'm not sure about that," I respond.

"Hey, what are you all talking about," Yolanda asks as she walks up.

"I'm so happy to see you," I admit knowing they will not continue the conversation in front church lady.

"Nice outfit, but it looks extremely expensive. Are you spending all your money shopping?" Yolanda questions.

"Hell, nay. I'm spending all Jason's money and banking mine," I inform.

"You went from dating an educated man that wanted to uplift the urban communities too dating a man whose occupation causes devastation to the communities," Yolanda state.

"Let's get something straight that educated man was a two timing dog and Jason is a piece of ass with cash to waste. Not all of us are looking for a husband," I respond.

"Wait a minute this is getting to serious," Carrie interrupts.

"Don't sweat we have the same conversation at least two or three times a week," I disclose.

"You know I love you and only want the best for you," Yolanda blurts out.

"I know that's why I let you get away with it. Group hug and another round of drinks on Jason," I announce as we embrace in a group hug.

Chapter 25

On the ride home after dropping Carrie and Yolanda off, I contemplate over Brittany's advice. So, far her advice about how to milk Jason has been dead on. Lying to him about my true feels is not the problem, it's the oral thing.

"R U up," I text to Jason.
"Heading home," he text.
"Come over," I text.
"R U alone?" he text.
"Yes & horny 4 u," I text.
"C u in 10," he text.
"More like 20. Wait until he finds out my car want go past 60 miles," I laugh to myself.

Let me set the stage. Four shoots of Patron than upstairs to freshen up. Another three shoot before he arrives. By the time he makes it over the shoots should be kicking in.

"Come on in," I greet opening the door wearing nothing but some lacey thongs with my large breast standing at attention.

"So you're horny for this dick," he says closing the door and grabbing his balls. "She may be drunk as hell but, damn her fine ass is making my dick hard," he thinks to himself.

"From the bulge in your pants I can tell you're also horny," I reply.

"So what you're going to do about it?" he question.

"Let me show you," I comment as I unfasten his pants stroking his dick. I'm not sure what compel me to drop to my knees. His dick is staring me in the face. The next thing I know it's in my mouth. I'm glad the shoots are fully kicking in, because this is totally gross.

"Ohhhh, ohhhh, oooooooohhhhhhhhhh, that feels so good," he yell out. "I can't believe this is happening. I've been waiting for her to give me head, but didn't know how to ask. What more can I ask for in a woman. Freak in the bed and a lady in the street," he's thinking to himself.

"I hope it was enough to seal the deal, because that's all I can stand," I'm thinking to myself on my third gage.

I stand up engaging him in a deep tongue kiss. I leap up on him wrapping my legs around his back as he holding on to my ass.

Still kissing I quickly carry her upstairs. I lay her on the floor at the top of the landing. The second I move the crouch of her thongs over my dick instantly penetrates her hot wet pussy.

With my legs still wrapped around his back I grab a tight clutch around his arms. I'm thrusting my hips in an upswing for deeper penetration of his dick on his down strokes.

"Fuck this pussy.   It's all yours," I moan loudly.

"Damn this some good pussy," he blurts out.

"Baby, slow your strokes to make it last longer," I suggest.

"Your pussy is so good I can't help myself," he admits.

"I love feeling you inside," I claim.

"I love being inside of you," he reply.

"Oooooooooooohhhhh," I scream out as he rams is dick in deeper holding it there as his body stiffens up.

"This is all your fault," he blames.

"What you mean my fault?" I ask.

"That surprise blow job over excited me. I truly appreciated and enjoyed it, but what brought that on?" he question.

"We hung out at your boys club tonight. While, watching other couples made me miss you. I don't think I ever expressed how much you mean to me. I love being around you. I love all that you do for me. I love you for being a good man. I love everything about you. To sum it up, I love you," I lie.   "The truth I love your money," I think to myself as we continue kissing.

"Wow, I had no idea you felt that deeply for me," he happily respond before engaging her in a kiss.   "You're ready for another round?" he asks.

"Let's take this in to the bedroom. I do not want get a carpet burn on my back," I suggest.

He is completely naked when we reach my bedroom. I lay across the bed holding my legs out. He gently slid my thongs off.

With a strong hold on her legs I pull her butt to the edge of the bed. I open her legs wide out and kneel between them. I insert two fingers in her pussy and slowly thrusting them in and out.

I tighten my pussy muscles around his fingers as I gyrate to the motion of his strokes. An arousing rave of passion overcame me the second his tongue flicks across my clit.

I can feel her body tremble with excitement as I lick and suck on her clit, while I slowly finger fuck her. The second I feel her legs beginning to shake I pull my fingers out. I quickly stand up with her legs pressing against my chest and a tight grip around her thighs causing her butt to be lift off the bed.

By him having a tight hold of my legs and my butt being elevated off the bed is rendering me helpless as his fully erect dick slide inside my pussy.

"Yeeeeessssss," I scream out in pleasure from every powerful stroke of his dick.

"Damn, your pussy is hot and wet. My dick feels good up in your pussy," you bellow back.

It must feel good to him, because I keep seeing the minutes slip away on the clock off the cable box. He releases the tight hold on my thighs causing my limp legs to slide down his side.

With my dick still inside her tight wet pussy I climb into bed forcing her body to the center. I lean in to suck on her breast while I continue fucking her missionary style.

I allow myself to become powerless to his sexual needs. I let him take complete control. For the next thirty minutes my body moves in the rhythm of his strokes for every position he chooses.

While we're in the doggie style I lightly tug on her hair as my dick explodes inside her pussy. Both our bodies collapse to the bed from exhaustion.

"That was magnification," he blurts out.

"It was," I agree as I squirm from under him.

"Your car is a piece of shit," he burst out laughing

"It gets me from point A to Z. I'll get a new car after graduation," I reply throwing a hint.

"I don't think it will last until you graduate. We can start looking for a car when we get back from Las Vegas," he divulges.

"Wow, that's the best Christmas present. You are too good to me. When?" I squeal out.

"The car is not a Christmas gift," he stutters.

"I'm not talking about the car. We're going to Vegas. I've never been on a real vacation. When are we going?" I reply.

"We're going for New Year's Eve. From the 29th until the 2nd of January," he responds.

"First thing Monday I'm putting in my vacation time," I reply engaging him in a kiss.

"By the way I'm in love with you," he informs being thrill to see her reaction is for the trip and not the car.

"Once again Brittany is right. I'm getting a car on top of a trip to Vegas for giving him head. That shit was nasty, but effective," I'm thinking to myself as I snuggling in his arms.

"I truly love this woman. Damn she's beautiful, sexy, intelligent, and in love with me. She is my queen and her car needs to reflect that. There is nothing I wouldn't do to keep her. I'll break the news to her in the morning that my mother is expecting our presence for Christmas dinner," he thinks to himself as Spring peacefully lay in his arms.

"As I lay with my eyes close all I can think about is what color car do I want? Red is sexy. Nay I'm sexy enough. Orange and yellow are too bright for me. I don't want anybody to think I'm fun loving or joyful. Tan is too simple for me. I'll never do simple again in my life. White is plain and purple is original. I'm definitely not either one of them. Green is traditional. I hate traditions. Blue is dependable. I'm not out to help anyone but myself. Silver is elegant. I can do elegant. Black is powerful, classic, elegant, and not easily manipulated. Black it is. Now I have to figure out what kind of black car best suits me," I'm going over in my head as I doze off.

Chapter 26

One suitcase for my shoes, two suitcases for my clothes, and a carryon for my makeup and accessories. That should hold me for five days. I'm going to make the best of this trip, so when I walk out this door the real me stays at home and the fake good girlfriend goes on this trip.

Once the plane climbs above the clouds my imagination begins running wild. As I stare out the window looking at the clouds, an image of my mother in a beautiful snow white gown with the most amazing pair of wings and a halo lightly hovering above her head appears. My eyes are becoming heavy as I trying holding on to that image.

She gracefully flies over to my window with a smile on her face placing one hand on the window. I press my hand on the window and our fingers match perfectly. The glow surrounding her presence radiates a calm peaceful warmth that's tingling every inch of my soul.

There is not one word spoken but I can feel her love running through ever fiber in my body. I doze off dreaming of me tightly holding onto her hand as we skip across the clouds. I sleep for most of the four hour flight.

"What were you dream about?" Jason asks as I'm waking up.

"I don't remember. Why you ask?" I question not willing to share.

"You grabbed hold of my hand and begin smiling in you slept," he replies.

"I'm assuming it had to be about you if I grabbed your hand," I lie.

"That's comforting," he state as he leans in for a kiss.

"Cut that out you two. We will be landing soon," his sister jokingly whisper from the seats directly behind ours.

"Mind your own business," he responds kissing me one last time.

We head straight to the hotel after picking up the rental car. The energy from the magnificent sights of the Las Vegas strip is exciting.

The aquatic performance from the water fountain in front of the Bellagio Hotel is mesmerizing. The eerie but beautiful display of bright colorful hand-blown glass flowers on the ceiling immediately caught my eyes the moment we enter the hotel's lobby. The hotel still has Christmas decorations up. I affectionately embrace him as we walk to our room. My anticipation of exploring all the sights this hotel and Las Vegas has to offer makes me appreciate being here with him at this moment.

Our whimsical dual green and plum decorated deluxe king room appears to be inspired by their botanical gardens. The entertainment center has a generously stocked mini-bar. After figuring out how to operate the automatic drapery the large picture window displays a breath taking view of the city. How sexy to have a bathroom with a soaking tub and a glass enclosed shower.

After everyone's arrival Brittany, Shannon, Jason, and I decide to explore the strip. The lights from the hotels attractions give the strip a different vibe after the sunset. Since, the men have to leave so early tomorrow morning we're doing the entire 4.2 mile strip by way of a horse and carriage instead of walking.

The carriage makes stops so we can watch the volcano erupt at the Mirage hotel and the pirates' battle at Treasure Island Hotel. I'm mentally marking all the spots I plan to check out. From Brittany's facial expression the sight of the Fashion Show Mall excites her.

Watching the water show in front of our hotel is our last venture for the night. I notice Fran and Lamont watching us, so I engage Jason in a very sensual kiss. By the end of this trip I'm hoping to have his sister convince that our relationship is real, make Lamont realize that I don't want his hoe ass, and ensure that Jason will let me pick my own car.

"I want to thank you for this," I honestly admit.

"Trust me Babe, there was no way I was bring in a new year without you," Jason responds.

"You're too good to me," I reply wrapping my arms around his neck and kissing him until the elevator reaches our floor.

We commence to stripping the moment our room door closes. He picks me up carrying me across the room to lay me across the bed. He immediately buries his face in my chest taking turns sucking on my breast. I open my legs wide to welcome his fully erect dick inside.

My dick penetrates her wet pussy as I hold tightly on her breast taking turns sucking each nibble. The raw passion I have for this woman is unimaginable.

We fuck like dogs in heat for the next fifteen minutes.

"Sorry about the quickie. I'm stressed about tomorrow's trip," he apologetically explains.

"Everything is going to be ok," I soothingly reply.

"Just worried, because these are new guys and we are entering their territory, which gives them a big advantage if the deal goes sour," he admits.

"I doubt if your boys would put you in a dangerous situation. You're going to take care of business and then we are going to bring in another new year together," I comment hoping to ease his worrying.

"You're right. I'm worrying about nothing," he responds.

"I love you," I whisper in his ear.

"I love you too," he whispers back.

"What time is it?" I ask being wakened a couple of hours later to the sound of Jason scuffling around the room.

"Too damn early in the morning! It's still fucking dark outside," he complains.

"The early bird catches the worm," I reply.

"Yahh, Yahh, Yahh. What do you have planned for the day?" he grumbles.

"I might go shopping with your sister when I finally roll my ass out of bed," I answer.

"I'll leave you some money on the dresser just in case you decide to," he replies happy to hear that his woman and sister are bonding.

"Thanks baby. You have a save trip," I smile holding the blanket up to expose my naked body.

"On that note, I'm out of here before you start trouble," he comments while scrambling to open the door.

"Put the do not disturb sign on the outside of the door," I request.

Chapter 27

Let me get up to go work out. I need to mentally prepare myself before hanging out with his sister. If it wasn't for Jason treating his sister's opinion as the gospel I would sleep in. My actions today could destroy my plans for a new car. I have to make sure she doesn't pick up that I only think of her bother as my cash cow.

"Yea. Hurry your ass up so we can hit the mall?" I demand while knocking on Brittany's hotel door.

"I'm coming. Perfection is not an easy task," Brittany yells out as the door to her room opens.

"Fran is meeting us in the lobby," I mention.

"Meeting us for what?" she ask with a puzzled look on her face.

"She's going to the mall with us," I reveal.

"Why did you invite his sister?" she question.

Karma is a Bitch

110

"She asked and since, I'm playing the role of a real girlfriend I thought it was the correct answer," I reply.

"Fran is setting your ass up. You know she's going to see if your motives are genuine or not for her brother," she note.

"I know. I got this covered," I respond.

"This would look good on you," Fran suggest

"It would, but have enough tops in that color," I hint.

"We've been shopping for the last hour and you haven't bought a thing. Didn't my brother leave you some money?" she asks.

"Yes, but I have more than enough clothes at home," I reply.

"Why did you come if you're not buying anything?" she question.

"I thought it would be an excellent opportunity for us to spend time together without being in large group," I claim.

"You're right," she replies being shocked at my answer.

"Good answer," Brittany type in a text message.

"Playing the role of a loving faithful girlfriend is hard work. It's agonizing trying not to buy a thing at a mall with all the money he left. I can't afford for his sister to know that I'm attracted to the material things he provides for me," I'm thinking to myself.

"For the next couple of hours Fran is acting like we're close friends. Know she's suggesting we go out to dinner before heading back to the hotel. Oh, please let this day end before I slip up and the truth comes out," I'm screaming in my head.

Chapter 28

"On my way home. Ready to bring in another New Year. Love you," Marcus text his wife while leaving an early New Years Eve celebration with another one of his girlfriends.

"Who the fuck is Brittany," his wife text.

"The hell if I know," he text.

"Are you fucking the bitch," she text.

"Fucking who," he text.

"Don't treat me like a motherfucking fool. Are you fucking that bitch?" she text.

"I don't know anybody named Brittany," he text.

"Someone from a 248 # keep playing on my phone," she text.

"What makes you think I know who's playing on your fucking phone?" he text.

"Is it the same number under Brittany in your phone's contact list?" she text.

"What the hell is your problem?" he text.

"Stupid ass, I know your pin number. I went through your cell. Tell your bitch to stop calling me," she text.

"What the fuck is going on? You know I spend the holidays with my wife and kids," he says leaving a message on Brittany's voicemail.

"Call me ASAP," he text Brittany.

"What the hell is your problem," he text her.

"Pick up your fucking phone," he says leaving another message on her voicemail.

"Bitch, leave my wife alone," he text her.

"What the fuck is wrong with you," he text her.

"Why the hell are you call my wife," he text her.

"Bitch, answer your fucking phone," he said leaving a message on her voicemail.

He drives over to Brittany's house, but doesn't see signs of anyone being there. He gets out his car to walk around the house. He's able to peek into a garage window, since the blinds are partially closed. He can see that Spring's car is the only one in the garage.

"I'll be back to deal with her ass," he mumble.

Chapter 29

If I didn't know any better I would believe they are all related by blood. This meeting up before we go anywhere is fucking ridicule. Our first night we had to hang out in the casino until everyone arrived. Last night when the men got back we meet up for drinks. This morning we all meet for brunch and again for an early dinner. Now we're waiting for everyone to show up before heading to the club? I hope it's not going to be like this the entire trip!

We finally make it to the club. I know from the smile on Jason's face as he helps me out my mink coat that he's a proud man. I'm wearing a silver beaded form fitting dress to show off my hour glass shape. The low square cut neckline of the dress and perfect jeweled choker necklace embellishes my large perky breast. My Michael Kors silver stilettos intensify my toned legs. He holds me by the waist as we're escorted to our VIP section.

"Damn, you are absolutely stunning," he compliment.

"Just a little something my man picked out

for me," I said twirling around for him to view the whole package.

"He has an eye for what looks good on you," he happily state.

"He definitely does," I reply smiling.

I'm glad they purchased a VIP section at Pure nightclub in the Caesars Palace hotel. The place is jammed pack and it's only ten o'clock. This nightclub is something straight out the movies. The decor is a pure white theme, which is allowing the color lights to vibrantly reflect off.

We have a good view of the dance floor, several celebrities VIP sections, and the stage where the guest artist is expecting to perform. We're starting with two bottles of Champaign, a couple of rounds of drinks, and a tray of finger foods.

Just before midnight our waitress brings 4 additional bottles of Champaign. The DJ cuts off the music for the countdown to midnight.

"Ten, nine, eight, seven, six, five, four, three, two, one," we yell out while holding our glass of Champaign out in preparation for a toast.

"Happy New Years," is all you can hear throughout the club.

"Happy New Years my love," he whispers in my ear.

"Happy New Years. Thank you for a wonderful year and I look forward to many more," I whisper back before engaging him in a passionate kiss.

"Maybe this is as good as it's going to get,"

I thought to myself while cuddling in his arms kissing to bringing in the New Year. "He's not bad looking and has a decent body. I can't complain about the sex, since I only have one other person to compare him too. He loves the ground I walk on and his wallet is wide open for the taking. It could be worst. I could have been a retard and took Darrell's cheating broke ass back. Guess it want hurt to accept this as a real relationship," I ramble on in my head.

For the next four we party our asses off. After returning back to the hotel Jason and I stroll thru the conservatory and botanical gardens like two love birds. We talk, laugh, and dance to no music around the explosion of colors and radiate scents from the exceptionally gorgeous plants, flowers, and trees that are thoughtfully arranged to inspire the full holiday splendor. When we get back to our hotel room we make love until sunrise.

It's not until up around two in the afternoon I wake to the faint sound of my cell phone ringing.

"What's going on?" I ask.
"Meet me downstairs!" Brittany requests.
"Only if it includes food," I reply.
"Ok, the Café Bellagio in fifteen minutes," she suggest.
"Give me at least thirty minutes to shower and put a look together," I respond.

When I arrive to the restaurant Brittany has already ordered me a strong cup of coffee and strawberry Belgian waffles.

"Thanks," she acknowledges.

"You're lucky I need something on my stomach," I mention.

"I think you have Fran totally convinced that you're genuinely in love with her brother," she states.

"What make you say that?" I ask.

"All night at the club she kept looking in your direction. When we got back to the hotel I noticed her staring at the two of you acting like two love sick puppies in the garden. Hell, if I didn't know your real intentions I would think you and Jason are a real couple," she reply.

"Enough of the small talk, what is it that you really want to talk about?" I ask.

"Girl when I got back to our room my cell phone was ringing. It stopped just as Shannon was about to answer it," she says.

"I bet it was that damn Marcus," I reply.

"Yea. I had 30 missed calls, 57 text messages, and 25 voicemails from that motherfucker," she reveals.

"What the fuck did he want?" I question.

"I'm not sure. My phone fell in the only cup of water in our room when I snatched it from Shannon. He was pissed the fuck off. He wants me to end this the moment we get back. He was bitching about me not taking his offer to help," she discloses.

"So what are you going to do?" I ask.

"Go get me a new phone," she answers.

"I wasn't talking about your phone. What are you going to do about Marcus?" I question.

"I'm going to cut his ass loose the moment I get home," she admits.

"Want that jeopardize your deal with his brother," I ask.

"Oh well, if his brother backs out I'll take his ass to court," she claim.

"I have some money stashed away if you need it," I offer.

"Thanks," she replies.

Chapter 30

Jason is in the shower when I get back to my hotel room. I'm hoping that we can spend some time together without it turning into a group outing.

"Hey, baby. How about us hanging out on our own?" I ask while staring at him through the glass enclosed shower.

"I can't hear you. Come a little closer," he replies.

"How about us hanging out on our own!" I ask again.

"I still can't hear you. You might need to come in to talk with me," he suggest.

"Your ass can hear me. If you want me to join all you have to do is ask," I state.

"I thought with all your education you would have gotten the hint," he jokes.

"I am still suffering from last night. I think a hot shower and fresh air without the group will help," I propose while stripping off my clothes.

"So you asking me to ditch my peps and hang with only you today?" he question,

"Yes," I reply as I enter the shower.

"If you can convince me then it's a deal," he agrees.

It never takes much too sexually arouse him. I engage him in a deep tongue kiss. He pins me to the shower wall and insert two fingers in my pussy. It doesn't take long for my pussy to moisten up.

I crouch down a little and ram my dick into her pussy. She responds by throwing her arms around my neck and wrapping her legs around my waist.

"Ohh, ohh, ooohhh, Jason," I yell out.

"Uuummmmmmm," he moans.

"I love feeling you inside of me," I moan.

"I love being inside your pussy," he moan back.

After a couple of minutes he pulls out, turning me face forward to the shower wall, and renter my pussy from the back.

"Whose pussy is this?" he asks.

"It's all yours baby," I answer.

We fuck for another ten minutes in the show before busting a nut.

"I bet your peps can't make your dick stand at attention!" I imply.

"Not at all," he agrees.

"If you ditch them I can promise that your dick will appreciate it when we get back,"

"You're on," he accepts.

We visit several sites that I saw our first night. He convinces me try on my first roller coaster. New York New York hotel has a roller coaster that can be seen off the strip.

Surprisingly the Big Apple Coaster is so much fun, we ride it again.

Next we catch a cab to the Madame Tussauds wax museum located in the Venetian Hotel. We're just like kids striking poses and taking picture of each other with the life like wax figures. After an hour and half we venture inside the Venetian Hotel, which gives me the feeling of what it's like in Italy. I'm able to lure him aboard one of their Old World gondolas boats. We enjoy the romance of a live serenade, while taking in the sights as we float along the Grand Canal path constructed inside the hotel.

We stroll down the Las Vegas strip shopping for souvenirs, while heading towards our last stop. A half scale replica of the world-famous France landmark, the Eiffel Tower at the Paris Hotel. The 460 foot glass elevator ride takes us to an observation deck that has a 360 degree view of the bright colorful lights off the strip. We go a few stories down to the Eiffel Tower Restaurant for a romantic dinner. We sit at a corner table with a window overlooking the water show in front of our hotel.

"Thanks. This was a wonderful day," I state.

"I have to admit. I'm glad we did our own thing," he replies.

We ordered several appetizers and a bottle of Pinot Grigio wine to share between the two of us. There is so many delicious items to choose from. I finally settle for the Grand Seafood Platter that includes Lobster, Shrimp, Crab, Oysters, and Clams. He has the Maine Lobster dinner. By the end of our meal and another bottle of wine we know it's time to go the moment we become touchy feeling.

Back at the hotel, at his request we stop at the bar to have a quick drink with the group. After playing catch up with them about the day's events we decide to call it a night. Jason orders two bottles of Pinot Grigio to be delivered to our room.

After a day in the fresh air a warm soothing bath will be good. Our wine arrives as I finish preparing the water in the big soaking tub. Since, the water is steaming hot I decide to enjoy a glass or two of wine. I walk back into the room with nothing on but my bra and thongs. Jason is sitting in the oversized love seat with the wine tray next to him.

"Damn, you are fine. Do you need me to close the curtains," he asks.

"No. The backdrop of the cities lights is sexually arousing," I admit.

"Come over here and sit on my lap," he insists.

"I want to do more then sit on your lap," I state as I climb in straddling my legs over him so we can be face to face.

"So tell me what else you plan to do," he question.

"Drink some wine," I reply giggling as I grab one of the bottles taking a swig.

"Your ass wants to crack jokes," he chuckle as he takes a swig.

We swap kisses as we drank the wine straight from the bottle. I'm taking a drink as he begins squeezing my breast through the bra. I dribble the last of the wine down my chest and he licks and sucks it off.

I unloosen her bra clasps, push her bra up, to bury my face in her boobs as a suck on each nipple one at a time. The gyrating motion of her body is making my dick rock hard.

"Raise up baby," he requests to quickly unfasten his pants and slid them under his butt.

"This is what I really want," I inform as I reach down to rescues his fully erected dick from his boxers.

"Now that's what I'm talking about," he excitingly says.

I push the string of my thongs to the side and slide his dick into my wet pussy. I hold on to the chair arm rest as I clutch his dick. Watching him bit his bottom lip confirms that he is enjoying it as much as me.

"That's it baby. Ride that dick," he loudly moans.

"My pussy loves riding your dick," I moan back.

"I'm enjoying every stroke, but it's time for me to take control of this," he demands.

With our bodies still being connected I scoot to the edge of the chair, with a tight grip on her back, I lower her to the floor, and continue fucking her missionary style.

"That's it baby fuck the shit out my pussy," I yell out.

"You mean my pussy," he state.

"OOOOoooooohhh, oooohhh," I yell out wrapping my legs around his waist.

"Uuummm, Ummmmmmmmm," he yell back.

I grab her legs, swing them over my shoulder, and slightly lifting her ass off the floor, to fuck the shit out her wet tight pussy.

"Here I come," I yell out as my legs began to shake uncontrollable.

"OOOOOOOooooooohhh," he moan as his dick explodes from the sensation of my orgasm.

We lay on the floor exchange wet sloppy kisses.

"The bath water should be ready," I mention as a squirm from under him.

I slid off my thongs, grab the other wine, both wine glass, and head for the bathroom. He speedily gets completely undressed and follows. He climbs in first and I climb in sitting between his legs.

"It would be nice to take our relationship to the next level," he brought up as we relax in the tub.

"What do you mean by that?" I ask knowing what he was talking about.

"You know what I'm talking about!" he state.

"Me moving in with you," I reply.

"Yes," he answers.

"It will happen when the time is right," I respond.

"How much more right do the time has to be?" he asks.

"We'll talk about that later. Let's just enjoy this moment," I suggest.

I wake up just as the sun began peeking. I decide to surprise him. Thanks to both of us sleeping butt naked helps me to carry out my mission.

I wake up to my dick hard and Spring sucking on it. This is how a man should start his day.

The moment that I notice he's up I swing my body placing my pussy in his face. The 69 position allows him to pleasure me at the same time.

I grab a hold to her ass as my tongue explores every inch of her pussy. I suck, kiss, and lick her clitoris as she kiss up and down my dick.

The moment I go back to sucking his dick he thrust his tongue up my pussy. His tongue feels so good that I engulf as much of his dick as possible. As much as I enjoying him eating me out, I'm ready to feel him inside of me. I lean forward grabbing his ankles. He inserts his hard dick into my pussy. I slowly rode his dick.

"Oooooooooh baby, he moans out.

"Your dick got my pussy on fire," I yell out.

"Baby, turn around so I can see your beautiful face," he request.

"Sure, I'll turn around so you can enjoy my boobs," I reply.

I turn around and go right back riding his dick. I lean in so he's able to suck on my boobs.

Her pussy feels so good, but it's time I run this show. I instruct her to get on all four, so I can ride her doggie style. I'm beating up her pussy so bad that her body is going limp. I continue fucking her until I bust a nut.

Chapter 31

Our flight is delayed due to severe weather in Nebraska. We all walk down to the Lucky Streak Lounge in the airport. They didn't choose this location because it embraces the mystique of the Vegas experience. They choose it because of the bar.

"What the fuck is that?" Lamont yell out when Jason removes his jacket.

"What the hell is your problem," Dean questions.

"Jason's t-shirt," Lamont replies pointing in our direction.

"I think its cutie. Whose idea was it?" Fran ask.

"It was all Spring's idea," Jason blurt out.

"You went with that lame ass shit. What grown ass man walks around with picture of him and his woman on a t-shirt!" Lamont sarcastically states.

"This doesn't happen too often, but I agree with Lamont," Shannon admits.

"The same goes for me," Dean adds.

"I wasn't expecting him to wear it. I plan to wear it when I go to work out. A few of the punks at the gym need to visually see that I have a man," I confess in Jason's defense.

"You're having problems with someone at the gym?" Jason question

"There are a couple of dirty old men that thinks someone looking for a sugar daddy," I throw out hoping it speeds up me getting my car.

"Are you sure I don't need to come up there?" he question.

"It's not that serious," I claim as I lean in to kiss him.

"I'm sorry I commented on your t-shirt. I would have kept my mouth shut to avoid seeing you two groping each other," Lamont states.

"Fuck you," Jason replies in laughter.

We sit laughing, talking, eating, and enjoying a few drinks for the next few hours. It's helping to ease the three hour delay for our flight, but it fucks up our arrival time.

We get in Michigan after midnight. There is no one else in site and everything is closed. If it wasn't for the other passenger on the plane we would have been the only people walking from the terminal to baggage claim.

"Spring, can you do me a favor?" Brittany asks.

"Depends on what it is!" I reply.

"I'm going to stay over Shannon house. Do you mind taking some my luggage home?" she asks.

"Not at all, but you will need to follow us to his truck," I reply.

"It looks like Fran verdict is in," she state looking in Fran's direction.

"I hope it's all good. I need a new car. Actually it's not that bad having him as a fake boyfriend," I admit.

"Sounds like you are caving in," she comments.

"I'm not caving in, I'm just accepting my current situation for the sake of getting a new car," I respond.

"You're stupid," she laughs.

"I have to admit the two of you proved me wrong," Fran comments to her brother.

"Wrong about what?"Jason asks.

"I didn't think it was going to work between you and Spring," she state.

"Why?" he question.

"You have to admit she nothing like the other bucket head woman you dated. I just thought with her being beautiful, intelligent, and ambitious that she might just be using you. But I can see that she truly loves you. I'm happy for you," she admits.

"Thanks that means a lot coming from you," he response.

"Here comes the luggage," I state walking up to them.

Chapter 32

For the past two nights Marcus drives down Brittany's block and parking in a spot with perfect view of her house. He cuts off the car lights and lay waiting to see when and who she comes home with

"I wonder what's on that bitch's mind. I bet she's been with another nigga the last couple of nights. Who the fuck do she think she is. Nobody gets away with cheating on my ass and disrupting my household. Let me see what this bitch's next move is," Marcus thinks to himself.

A little before two am in the morning on the third night the black truck that he has seen several times before pulls up. He watches as Spring and Jason emerge from the truck. He observes as they unpack luggage then disappear into the house. His mind races with all kinds of thoughts, as he stares at a sliver of light peeping through Brittany's bedroom window.

Chapter 33

After an hour of staring at the light from Brittany's bedroom window he decides to call the house. The first two phone calls ring until they go to voicemail. Knowing that Spring is in the house motivates him to keep calling back. By the twelfth phone call he becomes enraged that she's avoiding his phone calls on purpose. So, he calls again. This time he leaves a message.

"Bitch I know you are covering up for your girl. Tell that hoe Brittany to watch her back. Nobody treats me like a fucking fool and get away with it," Marcus blurs through the house from the answering machine.

"Spring was that motherfucker calling you a bitch," Jason asks.

"That what it sounds like," I respond as the phone begins ringing for the fourteenth time.

"Who the fuck is this?" Jason demand answering the phone.

"Listen bastard. This is not between you and me. Just tell that hoe Brittany her ass is dead," he angrily yell back

"Calling my woman a bitch and threatening her girl makes it my business. Bring your ass over," Jason inform.

"I don't have time to play with a fucking child," he responds before hanging the phone up.

Jason tries calling the number back but Marcus refuse to answer.

"Call your girl to warn her about that motherfucker and I'll call Shannon," Jason order.

Both Brittany and Shannon's cell phones are going straight to voicemail. They leave multiple voicemails and text messages about Marcus crazy ass. They decide to call it a night with the bedroom door open to listen out for Brittany. Jason places his loaded gun on the nightstand for easy access.

Chapter 34

The next morning Marcus is still impatiently waiting in his cold car for Brittany to return home. He isn't sure what his reaction might be when he sees her, but many thoughts of what he would like to do to her races through his mind. He completely blocks out the buzzing of his cell phone going off. He doesn't have time to deal with the bitching from his wife. That's a problem he will deal with after rectifying the current situation.

While, pulling up to her house Brittany is still relishing over her New Years vacation spent with Shannon. She powers up her phone with the anticipation of a ton of voicemails and text messages from Marcus. She know she will have to deal with him very soon.

Marcus notice Brittany pulling up to the house a little after 10 am driving in the car he bought her last Christmas and wearing the mink coat he gave her this past Christmas. Reality of him being played like a punk, while she spent time with another man set off a rage of betrayal and jealously.

As she opens the trunk of her car, she notices a text from Spring warning her about Marcus.

"Marcus is in a rage. Call when you are near, so Jason and I can be outside to watch your back," Brittany's reading as Marcus walks up on her.

"Bitch where there fuck have you been," he angrily demand.

"I wasn't with your ass," she loudly says hoping to attract some attention.

"You been out fucking some other nigga," he yell out.

"What does it matter to you? I'm not that motherfucking important to you. You have a fucking wife and other hoes," she yells back.

"You can forget about this shit," he says snatching her car keys. "What the fuck was you thinking calling my wife's phone on New Year's Eve? Bitch I know about the sneaky undermined deal you are trying to put past my brother," he disclose.

"First I don't know what the fuck you're talking about me calling your delusional ass wife. Second you can have this car. It's not worth dealing with your ass. Finally there's nothing you can do to stop the deal between me and your brother. My contract is solid. If, needed I will take his ass to court," she loudly reply.

"You dumb ass bitch," he yell out as he

punch her in the face.

Brittany screams broke the silence in the house waking Spring up. She ran to look out Brittany's bedroom window.

"Jason, get up. Marcus is outside beating up Brittany," Spring screams out rushing to put clothes on before heading outside.

Marcus' second punch to her face is so powerful that she loses her footing falling against the inside of the trunk. Without a second thought Marcus grabs her legs stuffing them into to trunk and slamming the trunk door closed.

He realizes the commotion has attracted attention. Without a second thought he jumps in her car. He's pulling out the driveway as Jason and Spring come running out the house.

"He pushed her in the trunk. I called the police," one of the neighbors shouts.

"Go get my keys," Jason yells out while aiming his gun for the back window.

By the time Jason drove down the block, there is no sign of Brittany's car.

"Brittany is missing. The motherfucker kidnapped her," I'm frantically yelling on the phone to Shannon as the police pulls up.

Angela Hairston grew up in the City of Highland Park, Michigan and graduated from the University of Detroit Mercy with dual degrees. Currently she is working on several other titles to follow "Permanently Etched In My Heart" and "Karma is a Bitch" series under Highland Park Publishing. In 2009 she made her publishing debuted as one of the premier authors in "Cosmos Anthology 2010", published by 3-Queens Publications, which introduced an excerpt from "Karma Is A Bitch".

To write author:
Highland Park Publishing
Attn: Angela Hairston
P.O. Box 724651
Atlanta, GA 31139

To email author
hairston@highlandparkpublishing.com

Follow on Facebook and Twitter
hairston@highlandparkpublishing.com

To contact the model/actress
Asia Mills
hairston@highlandparkpublishing.com

To contact the photographer/graphic designer
Anthony Thomas
Ecmanthony@gmail.com
www.anthonythomasphotography.com

Highland Park Publishing
Introduces titles written by
Angela Hairston

Permanently Etched In My Heart

Karma Is A Bitch
series

Yana's Tale

Ho Know Your Place

Richard Doe

Also a premier author in "Cosmos
Anthology 2010" published by 3-Queens
Publications

Everybody has a story and this is mine. My name is Selena Wright I am fourteen, and the oldest of three kids. I live in a very small city in the heart of Detroit, Michigan known as Highland Park and H.P. to its residents. The city spans one square mile down Woodward Avenue.

Most of the homes are huge and several are considered to be mini mansions. When we first moved into Highland Park, the neighborhood was gorgeous. The streets were lined with beautiful tall evergreen trees until they became infected and the city had to cut most of them down. Every store up and down Woodward Avenue was bustling with businesses and neighbors took pride in their homes.

Declining economy followed by poverty dramatically changed the city. Political corruption swindled away the city's funds. Most of the positions at the police department were held by relatives of H.P's most notorious residents. Gangs' criminal activities increased and flooded the neighborhood with drugs. Eventually the bustling businesses closed or moved out leaving abandoned reminisce of their presence.

My family live in the middle of the block in a four-story brick house with lead plated windows and a two ½-car detached garage.

The large front porch is built with limestone brick with three six feet long brick ledges. The inside of the house has solid oak wood detailing throughout. The brick fireplace in the living room is surrounded by built in oak cabinets with a mantel covered with family pictures.

My father had an entertainment room built to accommodate his 72' inch screen television with surround sounds. The downstairs half bathroom is located under the front stairway. The front stairway leads to an oversized upstairs hallway. The back stairway in the kitchen leads up to the second floor hallway. One of the four bedrooms is transformed into a computer room. My bedroom is the second largest room on the second floor. My brothers have a sunroom off their bedroom that's filled with an electric train set. My father has a bathroom in the master bedroom, while I'm left to share the large upstairs bathroom with my brothers.

The huge basement has a half bathroom. When the weather is bad my little brothers are able to ride their bikes and skateboards in the basement. My father claimed himself a room that he turned into a carpentry workshop. They love the basement, while I find it creepy. The saw dusk from my father's workshop attracts centipedes, which creeps me out.

I grew up in a happy loving household until my fourth grade year. It was a month after summer vacation ended. My mother was stopped at a red light behind a semi-truck when a pickup truck driven by a drunk driver rammed into the back of her car at eighty miles an hour. The impact pinned the entire front half of my mother's car under the bed of the semi-truck. Her head exploded when the rear bumper of the semi-truck trailer came crashing through the car's front window. The police had to remove portions of my mother's flesh and hair from the bumper and under the bed of the trailer. The police determined that she died on impact and never saw it coming.

I still remember that day clearly. It was the first time I ever saw my father shed tears. I was sitting on the living room window seat reading Green Eggs and Ham to my brothers Milton and Dwayne when a police car pulled up in our driveway. We went running to the front door when we heard my father scream. He was kneeling down on his knees crying. My brothers and I instantly hugged him and began crying. His tears silently told the story. My mother has gone to heaven and is never coming home.

My mother was the glue that held our family together. She was the one that planned all holiday and birthday celebrations. The first year without her was emotionally hard especially the holidays and birthdays, because they reopened the wounds of her death. The next four years my father raised us by himself. I helped out with my little brothers as much as possible. The first two years I had to initiate putting up holiday decorations, planning birthday parties for my brothers, and back to school shopping. As time passed, it became a lot easier to handle.

My mother was a beautiful black woman. Her grandmother from her father's side was an Indian. With her straight black hair and dark chocolate skin tone, she looked more like a Cherokee Indian instead of a black woman. Her small body frame hid the fact that she was a mother of three. When she talked, it was if she was singing. Everyone that crossed her path have only good stories about her.

My father could pass for a white man. His father was white and his mother was a light skin black woman. He is extremely light skinned, tall, and stocky with sandy curly hair. He has deep dimples in his cheeks and chin. His thin pink lips and slightly pointed nose resembles a white man. He once had a comical personality, but after our mother's death, he became very withdrawn.

I inherited my good looks from the unique combination of genes. I am 5-feet 3-

inches with a 136-pound athletic body perfectly packed in a size 2. My tan skin has a red under tone which gives the appearance of always having a suntan. My perfectly arched eyebrows enhance my brown eyes. I have my mother's cute nose and full lips. My long black hair reaches down to my bra clasp. Both sides of my family come from a long line of women with beautiful legs. Thanks to my skin tone, I get away without wearing pantyhose on my sexy legs. My friendly personality allows me to fit any crowd.

My brother Milton is eight-years old and one of the tallest kids in his third grade. He is the indistinguishable image of our father. My seven-year old brother Dwayne is starting second grade. He took after my mother's side of the family.

Several years after my mother's death my father began dating. I truly disliked this woman the moment he introduced her to us. His girlfriend Rita Harvey is four feet tall and shaped like an orange. She wears her clothes so tight that you can count the rolls of fat on her back. The three pounds of blonde weave piled on the top of her head blends in with her extremely thick foundation, three inches long eyelashes, five shades of blue eye shadow, and the brightest red lip stick I have ever seen.

Two weeks ago my father transferred to the afternoon shift. It left me home alone in the evenings with my brothers, so he moved his overly made-up girlfriend Rita and her three badass kids into our home. He thought it would be best for us to have an adult around the house in the evenings. Her two boys were the same ages as Milton and Dwayne so they moved into their room. Our computer room was converted into a bedroom for her ten-year-old daughter. From day one, I let it her known that I'm not conforming to her rules and regulations. That bitch moved into my mother's house!

Despite the changes in my home life, I am excited and ready to take on high school and all it has to offer. Highland Park Community High School is a fairly new but oddly constructed building that resides on an extremely small hill. From street level, it does not appear to be a school, but a white brick two story square shaped correctional facility without any windows. Once you enter the school, it feels as if you are completely cut-off from society. The smoke glass-ceiling window over the indoor garden and the glass framed main door entrance are the only connection to the outside. The first floor houses the main office, cafeteria, science labs, special elective classes, senior hallway, and the extension to the auditorium and athletic department. The second floor houses the vice principal's office, regular classes, and the library. The basement houses regular classes, special education, counselors, offices, and the school store.

I'm embarking on this new journey with my three closet friends. My babysitting partner Leslie Roberts has been my best friend since kindergarten. She's 5-feet 6-inches, with shoulder length hair, brown skin, big beautiful brown eyes, and the baby of seven siblings. Her witty personality makes her stand out in any crowd. We started our babysitting business a year ago with one customer and have grown to 9-regular customers.

Baron Smith is good-looking and very soft spoken. His rich black skin tone perfectly enhances his tall slim build. Because of his father and uncles influence, he thinks of himself to be a playboy. Our first grade teacher assigned us to become classroom partners. That was her way of forcing us to get along. I would never have kicked him if he had not pulled my braids.

Floyd Johnson is an average looking light skin brother with a stocky build that wears his hair in a long ponytail claiming it enhances his athletic abilities. He attended one of the other middle schools in the city. We met at a track meet between the schools. The summer of my fourth grade year through the school district combined middle school summer track and field program is when our friendship flourished.

I met Brandy Love in third grade when she transferred to my elementary school. She's an only child and her parents keep her extremely well groomed that deflects the fact that her left eye is lazy. She only befriended Leslie and I thinking it was a way to get Baron to notice her. Once she realized his ego was bigger than hers the quest for his attention faded.

My first two months as a freshman at Highland Park High School drastically changed my whole outlook on life. It's only the third week of school and I'm standing at my locker on the third floor in freshman hall when I witness my first shooting. My locker is at the end of a long narrow hallway. While exchanging books and talking with several other classmates an argument breaks out.

Derrick is a low-level weed dealer and bully that nobody likes. The word on the street is that he's looking for one of his foot runner's. He's accusing the runner of shorting him seven dime bags of weed. He sneaked into school to confront the boy at his locker.

"Were the fuck is my weed!" Derrick asks.

"I told you I did not take any of your fucking weed!" he answer with bass in his voice.

"Who do you think you are getting grim with? I should bust you in your motherfucking mouth!" Derrick reply.

"I didn't take your shit!" he responds.

"Listen here you punk motherfucker you better come up with my weed or the money by tomorrow. If not it will be your ass!" Derrick demand.

"What the hell do you mean by that?" he asks.

"Don't have my shit tomorrow and your scary bitch ass will find out!" Derrick threatens.

"Why wait for tomorrow I have something for you now!" he reply.

"That's more like it," Derrick responds.

The runner turns around and rambles in his locker. He unzips his book bag and pulls out a .38-caliber handgun. He quickly spins around pointing the gun at Derrick's head.

"What the fuck!" Derrick yells out.

"Who's the scary bitch now motherfucker?" he question.

Derrick is trying tried his best not to show the fear he's was feeling inside. He toughens up his voice and shout out, "If you shoot you better shoot to kill. Cause if I live your ass is dead!"

It looks as if the runner having a second thought. He was slowly lowering his arm then "Bang!" the gun goes off. Derrick eyes widen and his mouth open up as the look of disbelief flash across his face. For a few seconds no sound coming out of his mouth then he releases a screech of pain. He grabs his stomach as he falls to his knees. He grasps hold of a male student's pants as he started to lean over. The student panicked and started hitting Derrick's bloody hand until he let go. Derrick fell over on to his back. By then his scream turned into a loud distressful cry.

I slowly turn around with my hands covering my ears from the loud deafening sound only to seeing Derrick lying on the floor with a single gunshot wound to his stomach. The loud bang from the gun has me unable to hear all the screaming and crying. Although, I'm unable to hear a thing the smell of gun smoke looms in the air. The hallway is immediately becoming filled with students pushing their way down the hallway to see what happened.

Permanently Etched In My Heart

The runner is jumping around ranting. "Get the fuck up! Get the fuck up! I say get the fuck up! This is what your ass gets! I told you I didn't take any of your motherfucking weed! Motherfucker I guess you won't be coming after me now! Look at your bitch ass laying there on the floor! Who's the man now? What the fuck did I do? How am I going to explain this to my mother? All you had to do was believe me. You brought this on yourself. I'm going to hell! Your fat ass better not die on me! I want my mother!" he cries out.

Why am I not running or screaming? Why do my legs feel like two large blocks of cement? I can feel the crowd pushing up against me but they're unable to move me from my spot. Why am I just standing here in amazement and watching as Derrick lay on the floor begging for help? Why did I watch his stomach swell up until his t-shirt could not stretch any further? It's like a volcano. The blood is squirting through the fabric of his t-shirt and running down the sides of it. Is seems as if his cries are reducing to a gurgling moan as he spitting up blood.

Many of the kids are crying and screaming, while Derrick is laying here choking on his own blood. Why am I staring in his eyes and watching his soul fade away.

. The runner is shaking and crying hectically as he taking his last breath. He drops the gun and pushes his way through the crowd.

The jammed packed hallway causes the school security officers, police, and paramedics to reach Derrick after he took his last breath. Due to the chaos, the gunman was able to slip through the crowd and out of the building.

Immediately after the police finds out the identity of the shooter, they head over to his house to arrest him. His mother is home but has not seen him since he left for school this morning. They thoroughly search the house but are unsuccessful with locating him. While searching the garage one of the officers notice the family dog covered in blood. The officer follows the bloody paw prints straight to the dog's house. There they locate the gunman's lifeless body inside. He slit his throat and bled to death.

Because the murder happened at an inner city school, there is no grievance counseling for the students. The only thing we got is an early dismissal for that day. A week later, the school board implemented their crime prevention plan. Called for all doors except the main door to be chained and bolt locked from the inside during school hours, metal detectors installed in the main entrance doorframe, and the security guards equipped with handheld metal detectors.

With all the preparations and anticipations for homecoming, the murder became old news. It's amazing how much hype is put into the day knowing the last time we won a homecoming game was 10 years ago! The Saturday morning of the homecoming game start off with a small parade. It's beginning at one end of Highland Park marching up Woodward Avenue to the high school football field.

The football team leads the parade in the school athletic bus. I'm waving as Floyd and the football team rolls by. The high school cheerleaders and a band combined of students from all three middle schools march behind them. They are trailed by floats from the freshman class, sophomore class, junior class, senior class, and all our school organizations and clubs. The last float is carrying the homecoming king, queen, and the royal court. Our high school pom-pom squad and marching band follows behind the last float.

This is my first homecoming game and I'm thrilled. I don't know a thing about football, but the enthusiasm from the crowd is mind-blowing. It's exciting just to be part of it. The whole homecoming experience is totally different for Floyd. He is the first freshman to make our schools varsity football team.

The stadium is packed. I could feel the bleachers swaying whenever the crowd began stomping and cheering the football team off. It doesn't matter that we lost the game I'm still looking forward to the homecoming dance tonight.

Leslie and I are getting dressed for the homecoming dance over Brandy's house since, her mother is dropping us off. I'm wearing wore a red knee length dress, a pair of red flats, my long hair is down with curls at the end, and clear lip-gloss as my only makeup. Leslie wearing a long black dress, a pair of black pumps, her hair straight back, and dark red lipstick. Brandy wearing a tight black leather dress, a pair of snakeskin heels, a fresh short haircut, and enough make-up for all three of us. Brandy's father follows us out the house taking pictures as we leave for the dance.

The homecoming committee did a terrific job transforming the cafeteria into a ballroom with decorated balloons in our school colors. Tables draped with royal blue table clothes and white balloon center pieces surrounded an area cleared for the dance floor. Students from our school radio station D.J. the party.

(Excerpt from)
Permanently Etched In My Heart

I danced and talked with my peeps the whole night. We were having a good time until a big ass fight broke out. A few punks ruin it for everybody. The crowd turns into a stampede of wild horses as students flee from the cafeteria. I find myself ducking from flying chairs as we run for the exit. We made it out of the building just as the police pull up.

A week later, Leslie and I skip school on Friday to attend a ditch party. Cathy who lives around the corner from Brandy is having the party over her boyfriend John's house. Cathy was doubled promoted twice and two years younger than any of us. She tries and does anything to fit in with a crowd. Her boyfriend John is seventeen, and a high school dropout. He stays across the train tracks with his mother in a big brick house in the middle of the block.

When we get to the house four of John's boys and five of Cathy's girls are already here. They all live in the neighborhood. John boys are members of Highland Park's gang that call themselves the Mob Squad. They pride themselves on terrorizing the neighborhood, robbing, and slanging drugs. Most of them either dropped out or were kicked out high school.

The first half of the morning is ok, but a little boring. All we're doing is talking and drinking. John cuts the music up loud and his boys' fire up blunts. Since, I hate the smell of marijuana, I grabbing a couple of beers and sitting on the front porch. Leslie takes a couple of hits from a blunt before following me outside. We sit on the porch, while they are doing whatever in the house. After a while we decide to walk up to the Coney Island restaurant on Hamilton Avenue to get something to eat. I see we are not the only ones skipping school. This place is packed with students. A few hours pass by the time we make it back to John's house. It looks as if most of his boys are gone.

"So, this is what goes on at a ditch party?" I ask Leslie.

"Pretty much. They drink, smoke, and some of them have sex," Leslie answer.

"Hell I could have stayed in school for this," I reply.

"Me too. This is my last ditch party," she respond.

"Girl, I have to piss like a race horse," I mention.

"I have to go too. Let's go back in," she admits.

The smell of weed is lingering in the air and the music seems to be even louder than earlier. Beer bottles, liquor bottles, cigar tobacco, and clothing was scattered all over the living room floor. Cathy and John are back in his bedroom. Two of her girls passed out on the big lounge chair they are sharing. Another one of her girls lying on the floor behind the couch wrapped in a blanket with one of John's boys. Another of Cathy girls on the couch sleep under a sheet partially covering her naked body and one in the downstairs bathroom passed out around the toilet.

"Should we go in there and wake her up?" I ask.

"Hell yea!" Leslie answer.

"Are you ok?" Leslie and I ask.

"Ney. I might be here for a while. There's another bathroom upstairs at the end of the hall," she slurs.

"Is there anything we can do for you?" Leslie asks.

"Nothing if you can't stop the room from spinning," she request.

Leslie and I look at each other before closing the bathroom door.

"You go first," Leslie insist.

"Thanks," I reply.

(Excerpt from)
Permanently Etched In My Heart

"Damn, this is a big ass bathroom. I hate that there is not a lock on the door. Even though the toilet looks clean, I'm still padding the toilet seat before squatting over it," I thought to myself.

Just as I'm finishing peeing the bathroom door swings open. I panic when I look up and see one of John's boys standing in the doorway. His pants are hanging with his dick sticking out.

"Get the fuck out of here!" I yell.

"Bitch I don't know who you yelling at!" he yells back.

"Get out before I start screaming!" I demand raising my voice.

"Go ahead. Nobody can hear you over the loud ass music!" he comments.

"Leslie. Leslie. Help," I scream.

I get up quickly and trying to pull my pants all the way up. Unfortunately, the bathroom is not that big. It happened so fast. He closed the door and rush me. The next thing I knew I'm on the floor and he is lying on top of me.

"I told your dumb ass nobody can hear you!" he says.

"What the fuck do you want?" I ask.

"You know what I want!" he says.

18

I start screaming as loud as I can, but the music is drowning my screams out.

"I know you don't think I'm not taking that pussy!" he command.

"No. Get the hell off me. This is not right!" I yell as I'm trying to fight him off.

"Shut the fuck up, Bitch!" he orders.

"Please don't!" I'm pleading.

"Begging is not going to help your ass. One day bitch you will thank me for this!" he claims.

"Go to hell you sick bastard. If you stop now I want report this!" I yell.

"To who? The police! Bitch I am related to the sergeant!" he says in a laughing tone.

"You will get yours one day!" I angrily states.

"I'm not worried about that," he laughs.

I continue screaming, while hitting him with my fist and kicking at him. He grabs me around the neck choking me with one hand while using the other hand to push my pants and panties down my legs. He then use his feet to force my pants and panties down around my ankles as I continue hitting him with my fist.

He takes a hold of my arms and uses one hand to pin my arms down above my head. During the struggle I cross my legs trying to keep him from penetrating me, but he forces his legs in between mine and prying my legs apart. My screams turns into cries as my body start trembles from the pain of him forcing his dick inside of me.

"Shit. You're a virgin!" he excitingly says.

Leslie came upstairs to see what was taking me so long. When she opened the door and saw that punk on top of me.

"What the hell is going on?" Leslie yells as she bust in.

"Who the fuck are you?" he asks.

"Get your motherfucking ass off her!" Leslie order as she jumps on his back and starts hitting him in the head.

"Bitch, get the fuck off my back!" he demands slinging her off his back. He pulls up his pants, run down the stairs, and out the front door.

The next thing I remember is sitting on the bathroom floor and Leslie holding me. We stay on the floor crying.

"You want me to call the police?" Leslie asks.

"No!" I reply tearfully.

"Why not?" she questions.

"How will I explain to my father that I was raped while skipping school?" I explain.

"Do you know who that was?" she questions.

"No, but I have seen him around," I answer.

"Let's go?" she instructs.

"I don't want to go home and I don't want anyone to find out," I request.

"You can stay over my house for the weekend. This will be our secret," she suggests in a sympathetic voice.

"Thank you. Do you mind if we stop by my house to pick up a few things?" I ask.

"Not at all," she answers. We left the party without alerting anybody. When we got to my house, I was glad to see that no one was there. I pack a bag and give my father a call at work to let him know that I'm staying over Leslie's house for the weekend.

When we make it to Leslie's house, I jump straight in the shower. I'm standing under the hot running water as I'm attempting to scrub the dirty feeling off my skin. No matter how hard I scrub I can't get rid of this feeling on the inside. All I want to do is cry.

The mental aspect of being violated is overpowering my physical pains of the attack. It hurt having something so precious stripped away so violently. I get out the shower, I put on my pajamas and place all my clothing from today in a plastic bag.

"Selena I warmed you up something to eat," Leslie announces as she enter her bedroom.

"Thank you. Leslie can you throw this bag in the trash?" I ask.

"Are you sure you want to throw away your clothes?" she question.

"Yes, I am sure. I don't want any remembrance of the assault," I answer.

"I understand," she replies.

When Leslie comes back upstairs, she finds me in the bed curled up in the fetal position. It's a damn shame the one time I decided to start the weekend early by skipping school is the worst mistake in my life.

With Highland Park being so small it doesn't take long before the rumor gets around school and I find out my rapist name is Charles Singleton. He was recently released from a juvenile boot camp where he spent two years for a carjacking.

To keep my father from finding out I talking to a school counselor or report the rape to police is not an option. For the next couple of months I relive the attack every time I fall asleep. I wake up in a cold sweat filled with anger. The anger is turning into hate towards the punk that did this to me. I can use that feeling of complete utter hatred towards that punk to help me form a brick wall around my damaged emotions. The brick wall will hide any revealing emotions whenever the rumor is brought up.

I needed to make sure my denial story believable. I will act as if nothing has happened, hang with the same group of friends, kept my grades up, continued to attend school activities, and group social events. Every time I run into Charles if he says something rude to me, I going to cuss his ass and claim that his story was a lie. I am dropping off the track team to avoid running into him when I'm alone. I promised never to put myself in a compromising position like that again

The Thursday before our school Christmas recess is beginning. Leslie comes running up to my locker.

"Girl did you hear who was found dead this morning?" Leslie frantically asks.

Permanently Etched In My Heart

"No. Who was it?" I answer with a question.

"It was that punk motherfucker Charles Singleton. They found him dead in an alley. Somebody shot him in the face," Leslie discloses.

"That's what that punk deserved!" I happily reply.

At that moment, it feels like a ten thousand pound weight has been lifted off my chest. Luckily, I only had to deal with that punk Charles only for a couple of months. It's the best Christmas present that anybody could ever give me. I would love to meet the person that sent that motherfucker to hell!